PIPER DAVENPORT

Road To FREEDOM

DOGS OF FIRE MC BOOK #10

DOGS OF FIRE
PIPERDAVENPORT.COM

Cover Art
Jack Davenport

ISBN-13: ISBN: 978-1-962938-09-9

Liz Kelly:
Thanks again. Your insight is always so spot on! You keep
this up, you're going to be on my permanent BETA list.
You're welcome!

Jack Davenport:
What can I say? You're perfection on legs. I love you more
than life.

Brandy:
Thank you for keeping the characters and timelines right!

Mary:
Thanks for the multiple read throughs!!!

Gail:
Thank you for your eagle eye!!! You're amazing!

Get ready to fall head over heels! Road to Peace is another page turner of alpha brilliance from Davenport. I fell in love with every single page and spent the last few wishing the book would never end! ~ Harper Sloan, NY Times & USA Today Bestselling Author

Piper Davenport can write one hell of a sexy biker! I can't get enough of the Dogs of Fire MC series ~ Geri Glenn, author of the Kings of Korruption MC Series

All it took was one page and I was immediately hooked on Piper Davenport's writing. Her books contain 100% Alpha and the perfect amount of angst to keep me reading until the wee hours of the morning. I absolutely love each and every one of her fabulous stories. ~ Anna Brooks, Contemporary Romance Author

ROAD TO PEACE was an incredible, page turning ride! If you're looking for a take-charge alpha hero who'll protect his heroine at any cost, then you HAVE to read Hatch and Maisie's story! I was swooning from the moment that badass biker stepped on the page! ~ Sybil Bartel, Author of the Uncompromising Series

This is one series I will most definitely be reading!! Great job Ms. Davenport!! I am in love!! ~ Tabitha, Amazeballs Book Addicts

For Harper Sloan
You know why!

ONE

Remington

"**9**-1-1, WHAT'S YOUR emergency?"

"There's a man trying to break into my apartment," I whispered as I hid in my bedroom closet. "His name is Vitaly Popov and I have a restraining order against him."

My phone buzzed, and I checked the screen. I had been texting back and forth with my friend, Grace Lundy, when Vitaly showed up at my door. Sending a quick note back that I was hiding, I put the phone back to my ear and listened for instructions.

Another bang against my door made me jump and I let out a quiet squeak.

"Ma'am?"

"I'm here," I whispered.

Today could only have been classified as a shitty day. Actually the past four days, really. The shittiest. Grace and

I had both been hired as paid interns for the Portland Ballet Conservatory, and it gave us an amazing opportunity to dance with some of the best dancers in the world, including Vitaly Popov who had been visiting from Russia.

At least, I thought it was an amazing opportunity.

However, Vitaly had cornered me in the practice room, and I hadn't been fast enough to escape, so I'd tried to talk my way out.

Unsuccessfully.

He'd slammed me against the mirror, the barre digging into my back, and forced his mouth on mine. I'd hit, bit, clawed at him with no luck, until Grace had walked in just as he ripped my leotard and I was finally able to shift and get a knee in his dick. But he still had enough of a grip on me to smash my face against the mirror, drawing blood as I bit through my lip.

Grace yelled, distracting him and helped me get away. I'd immediately reported the attack to the director of our ballet conservatory, and she dealt with the matter by firing me. Vitaly was a star, and I was a girl from a small town in Georgia. I was nobody. At least, as far as Director Walsh was concerned. If she actually knew who my family was, she'd be so far up my ass she wouldn't see daylight, but I'd used my grandmother's maiden name in all my paperwork, so she wouldn't know.

Grace had left PBC in solidarity with me, and I'd headed to the police station to file a report, then home to nurse my wounds.

Apparently, Vitaly had been served with the restraining order, because he yelled nasty things to me through the door in Russian. I knew they were nasty because I dated a Russian guy for about a minute, and the first words he taught me were the bad ones. How Vitaly knew where I lived was a mystery, but that made this situation even scarier.

"Okay, stay calm. What's your address?"

I swallowed, then whispered, "4200 Alberta, unit twelve."

"Where are you? Are you safe?"

"I'm in my closet," I whispered. "He's knocking on the front door and I'm scared he's going to break it down. Oh, God, please hurry!"

"Alright, ma'am, I've dispatched police officers to your address. Are you hurt?"

"No. No, I'm fine." Tears streamed down my face. "Just scared."

"What's your name?"

"Remi…ah, Remington Charles."

"Cool name."

"Thanks."

"Okay, Remi, stay calm, officers are three minutes out."

"He's still banging," I squeaked.

"Okay, honey, the police are close now. Take a deep breath and try to calm down."

I squeezed my eyes shut as Vitaly continued to pound on my front door. In the distance, I heard the muffled sound of sirens and the banging stopped. "I hear the sirens."

"Okay, hon, I'll stay on the line with you until the officers arrive."

"Thank you." I bit my lip. "The banging's stopped. I think he's gone."

"Officers are walking up your stairs. Can you open the door for them?"

"Um, sure," I said, and hauled my butt off the floor, easing out of my closet and heading to my front door. I checked the peephole and saw two men in uniforms, so I unlocked the door and pulled it open. "They're here."

"Okay, Remi. They will take it from here."

"Thank you."

I hung up and slid my phone into my pocket.

"Ma'am? Do you need me to call for an ambulance?"

"What?" I frowned, then remembered the bruises on my face. "Oh. No, these are from the other day. I reported them when I asked for the restraining order."

"Okay. Can you describe the man?"

"I have a photo," I said, and pulled up Vitaly's picture from PBC. "I also have the restraining order here. Let me get it." The paperwork was right by the front door, so I grabbed it and handed it to the officer. Just as I was taking the form back, Grace came running up the stairs, followed by her badass biker boyfriend, Flea. "Remi? Are you okay?"

"Don't move," the cop ordered.

Flea's hand went to his waist and I realized pretty quickly he was strapped.

"It's okay, they're friends," I rushed to say. All I needed was a shoot-out on my doorstep. "Thank you for getting here so quickly."

Grace had told me in passing that she was taking care of her grandmother who'd broken her leg, but we hadn't gotten much further into our personal lives. She was always pretty focused on the task in front of her and I was busy trying to keep up, so I was kind of surprised she was here.

Grace pushed past the officer, despite Flea's growl of warning, pulling me in for a hug. "Where's Vitaly?"

I shrugged. "I don't know."

"I have everything I need," the officer said. "We'll send a BOLO out for your assailant. We can put a car out front for a few hours—"

"No, she's going to pack a bag and come with us," Grace said.

"It's fine," I argued. "I don't think he's going to come back."

"Not really up for discussion," Grace bossed. "Pack a bag…enough for a few days. You're coming with us."

"Grace—"

"Don't argue with her," Flea said. "It's not worth the wasted breath."

Grace smiled. "What he said."

"Ma'am, what do you want to do?" the officer asked.

"I'll go with my friends," I said.

"Okay, my partner's searching the vicinity for Mr. Popov. We'll head out once you're gone."

"Thank you," I said, and went about packing a bag.

* * *

Finch

"No sign," Hatch said as I joined him back at the front of the building.

"Me neither," I said, and shook my head. "The message you gave him was ignored, apparently."

When Grace's friend had been attacked by Vitaly a few days ago, Hatch had said he roughed him up a bit and warned him to stay away. Almost broke his nose, definitely bruised it, but the asshole didn't listen.

"Little fucker. He's gonna regret that."

Hatch Wallace was the Sergeant at Arms for our motorcycle club, Dogs of Fire. I was a member and typically worked closely with Mack, our club's legal counsel, but tonight, I was at Hatch's place when my sister, Grace, freaked. And when Grace freaks, we all pay attention.

"Let's check on Gracie's friend," Hatch said, and I followed him up the stairs.

We passed a couple of beat cops and one of them turned and cocked his head. "Merrick Lundy, is that you?"

Hatch stalled as I faced the officer. "Who's asking?"

"Mike Watts."

I grinned. Mike had come up in the academy with my dad, but I hadn't seen him in years. It was impressive he even recognized me. "Hey, Mike. It's been a while."

Hatch's protective stance relaxed, and he continued up the stairs.

"What are you doing these days?" Mike asked.

"Law."

"Of course you are. Shit, you could always bring an argument."

I chuckled. "That's what I've been told."

"Well, good for you," he said. "You and your sister were always good kids. Sad about your mom."

My mom had killed herself ten years ago after taking Grace hostage, and it had been a nightmare. Particularly for my sister.

I gave him a chin lift. "Thanks."

"Gotta get back to it. Tell your dad I said 'hey' and take care of yourself."

"You too, man." I gave him a chin lift and headed up the rest of the stairs.

Where I froze.

Remington Fucking Charles.

Goddammit.

"What the hell are you doing here?" she snapped.

Apparently, she remembered me, too. Petite, blonde, and ample with both tits and ass, she was even prettier than she had been two years ago.

I smiled. "It would seem I'm saving you."

"You know my brother?" Grace asked.

"Merrick's your brother?" Remi asked, a look of horror crossing her face.

"Finch," I corrected.

Her head snapped to me. "What?"

"Finch. Not Merrick."

"Club name," Grace provided.

"You're part of the club?" Remi asked.

"Yeah, babe."

"Don't call me babe," she ground out. "Since when?"

"Recruit since I was eighteen."

I'd only recently patched-in, but I'd asked to be a recruit the second I'd turned eighteen. Unlike many of my brothers, I had a tight family unit, but my father was a police detective, so I'd had to wade into the pool of bikers with caution. For both them and me.

"Wait." She waved a finger in a circular motion toward me. "You weren't wearing your fancy vest last time I saw you."

"I was dressed for court last time I saw you."

"Court?"

I nodded. "I was defending a case."

"You're a lawyer?"

"Yeah."

"Of course you are," she lamented, dropping her head back. "What the fuck did I do, God? What? Huh? Is this my punishment? Okay, message received. I will never fuck some cute guy I just met in a bar ever again."

My sister's face was bright red as she tried to hold back her laughter, and I watched Remi in all her dramatic glory. Fuck me, this woman was still just as stunning as I remembered.

Hatch and Flea were doing their best to pretend they weren't listening, but Hatch gave me a fatherly eyebrow lift and I knew he'd expect some sort of explanation later.

He wouldn't get one.

Well, he wouldn't get *much* of one. What Hatch really wanted to know, was whether or not I respected her before, during, and after I fucked her. And I did.

The particulars weren't important…not to him anyway.

I studied the cuts and bruises on Remington's face and rage threatened to burst out of me. "You're the one Vitaly attacked?" I asked.

"How did you know about that?" Remi demanded.

"He was there," Grace said.

"What?" she squeaked. "How did I miss *that?*"

"He dropped Flea off…he didn't know who you were."

"God!" Her button nose scrunched up in despair. "Ain't that all a glorious cherry on top of my shit sundae."

God damn, her southern accent still made my dick hard.

"I hate to break up this reunion," Flea said. "But we should probably get you both back to your Grams'."

Grace nodded. "Yes. That would be good."

"You're still at your grandmother's?" Remi asked.

"Yes."

"I don't want to intrude, Grace. I can go to a hotel."

"You're not going to a hotel," I said. The thought of her at some dive motel, alone and exposed to god knows what made my skin itch.

"You don't really have a say in it," she countered.

"If Vitaly found you here, what would stop him from finding you at some shitty motel?"

"What makes you think it'd be a shitty motel?"

"Even if it was the fuckin' Ritz, he could track you down and then what would you do? You'd have no way of escape," I said. "Taking you back to my place."

She turned her scowl to me. "Like hell you are."

"It's either my grandmother's or my brother's," Grace said.

"You can both come back to my place," Flea countered.

I shot him a look of warning and I know he understood it, because he grinned.

Fucker.

"Can you stay with Grams, Merr?" Grace asked.

Our grandmother had surgery on her broken leg a little while ago, so we were all taking turns staying with her, so she didn't try to overdo anything.

"Flick's still there," Flea said.

I scowled at Flea. I didn't want him inserting himself into a situation that was between me and Remington, but I tried to soften my expression when I glanced back at her. Her chin was up in a challenging position and she couldn't have been more beautiful. I focused back on my sister. "If

Flick needs to leave, I can stay with Grams."

She smiled, standing on her tiptoes to kiss my cheek. "Best brother ever."

"Let's go, baby," Flea said to Grace, and grabbed Remi's bag.

"Give me a sec, yeah?" I asked, and Flea nodded, ushering Grace down the stairs, while Hatch followed.

I cut off Remi's escape and studied her. "How bad did he hurt you, Rem?"

"I'm fine."

"Not what I asked."

"Merrick—Big Bird—Tweety—whatever you call yourself these days…"

"Finch," I provided.

"Finch. I'm fine. I just want to forget this day ever happened."

"Did you get those cuts looked at?"

"Yes, but they're superficial. I have a few bruises, but I've been icing. I've had worse injuries dancing."

"I don't doubt it."

"Can I go now?"

"Not yet."

She rolled her eyes. "Merrick, I'm good. But if you don't step aside, I'm going to get in my car and drive to a hotel. This is ridiculous."

"Don't do that, Remington," I said. "Grace was worried enough to drag us all down here, so I'm getting the impression you're not being honest about the severity of the situation. You going to a hotel isn't going to happen."

"Well, neither is this conversation. Let me pass."

I sighed, knowing I'd get no further, and stepped aside. She walked down the stairs and I followed trying not to notice the graceful way her hips swayed as she headed toward my sister. Memories of her tight pussy covering my dick flooded my mind and I had to take a few deep breaths to keep from humiliating myself in front of my family.

Goddammit, one night with her hadn't been enough.

* * *

Remi

Flea took my bag from me and set it in the trunk of Grace's car. "Why is my bag in there? I'm driving."

"You've had a fright, Remi," Grace countered. "I figured you'd rather not."

"I'm good," I said.

"I'll drive you wherever you need to go," Merrick offered.

"That'll give me an even bigger fright," I mumbled somewhat under my breath.

Merrick chuckled, indicating it wasn't quite under my breath enough.

I cleared my throat. "I'm fine to drive, on *my own*," I said pointedly to Merrick. He stared at me, and the feelings I stuffed down two years ago flooded back again. I bit back frustration and met his eyes.

"I'm going to follow you."

I scowled. "Merr—"

"Not up for discussion, Remi," he bossed.

I grabbed his arm and pulled him away from Grace and Flea. "Merrick. Please. Will you just go home?" I whispered.

"Fuck, no."

I frowned. "Why not?"

He smirked and stepped closer to me. "You and I have some unfinished business."

That's what I was afraid of. "We finished our business two years ago," I countered.

"If you really think that, then you're high."

"Ohmigod, Tweety, you have no right to say that."

"You don't think so?"

"No," I snapped. "One night. That's all it was supposed

10

to be."

He crossed his arms. "And, in the morning, did you still feel that way?"

"Yes."

Merrick grinned. "Liar."

I *was* a liar. So much so, I could smell the smoke coming from my pants.

"You come back to my place, we can talk and if you still want me to fuck off, I'll take you wherever you want to go."

I squeezed my eyes shut. If I went with him, I'd fuck him, and that would not go well for me.

"I won't let you take advantage of me," he said, reading my mind and I gasped.

"Excuse me?"

"If you come with me, we'll talk. Nothing else."

I rolled my eyes.

"You can follow me to my place, or ride with me."

"Merrick."

"Finch," he corrected.

I narrowed my eyes and said, "Tweety."

He dropped his head back and laughed. "Come on, Rem, I have an extra helmet."

"I don't think this is a good idea."

"Now or later," Finch said. "But it's gonna happen, and I'm all about getting this kind of shit out of the way."

"Why?" I demanded. "We had our time."

He leaned closer. "Are you seriously still trying to tell me that that night meant nothing to you?"

"Was it supposed to mean *something*?"

Finch chuckled. "Not an answer, Rem."

"Look, I have no problem sitting down and having a conversation with you about all of this, but can we not do it tonight?"

"Kinda forgot you've had a shit day, huh?" He sighed. "Yeah, baby, we can wait."

I nodded and headed back to where Grace and Flea waited.

"You okay?" Grace asked.

"Yep. But, seriously, I'm going to drive, okay? I don't want to be without my car."

Grace faced Flea. "I'll go with Remi, honey. Do you mind driving my car?"

He nodded, leaning down to kiss her quickly. "I'll follow you."

Grace and I climbed into my car and she directed me to Flea's house.

Finch

BUZZING SEEPED INTO my head and I realized it was my phone. "Yeah?" I answered without looking at it.

"Merr, Remington's gone," Grace said.

I sat up and threw the covers off. "What do you mean, 'gone'?"

"I heard a car start up and knew something was wrong, so Flea checked out front and her car's gone."

"Goddammit, Grace."

"Don't 'goddammit Grace' me, big brother. You're probably the reason she's freaked."

"Is Flea tracking her phone?"

"He asked Booker to do it. But, honestly, I feel weird about it."

Booker was the VP of the Dogs and our resident computer expert.

I rolled my eyes as I dragged a pair of jeans on. "Get over that, sissy."

"She's entitled to her privacy, Merrick."

"Not if she's gonna run off in the middle of the fucking night," I countered.

"She's scared," Grace said. "I don't blame her."

"I don't either," I admitted. "So, if you let me go, I'll find her and tell her that."

"You can't leave Grams."

"I'm not at Grams'," I said. "Flick's still with her."

Flick was one of the club's oldest members and he had a past with my grandmother. One that was quickly being rekindled.

"Is Grams okay with that?"

"I think that's a rhetorical question."

Grace sighed. "Probably."

"I'm gonna go find Remi, okay?"

"Yes, but then you and I need to have a conversation about how you and she met."

"Do we, though?" I grabbed my wallet and the keys to my truck. If I had to force Remi into coming back to my place with me, then she'd probably feel safer in the truck.

"Yes, yes we do."

"Hanging up now," I said, and did so.

I fired off a text to Booker and headed out to the street where I'd parked my truck, sliding into the cab just as Booker responded to my text with the current location of Remi's phone. Why the fuck she was all the way up in Fisherman's Bar, I didn't know, but I headed that way.

Arriving at the park, it didn't take me long to find Remi's car, but she wasn't in it and this both worried and pissed me off. After shooting a text off to Cheese, one of the club's recruits, I dialed Remington's number and heard the faint sound of ringing to my right. Taking off that way, I kept the phone to my ear, but she never picked up.

Fuck. I hope I didn't find her phone shoved in a garbage can somewhere.

I dialed her number again and this time I heard a quiet hiss of irritation before the phone stopped ringing. I found her sitting on top of a picnic table her back to me, so I made my way to her. "Remi."

She let out a bloodcurdling scream and jumped off the table, spinning to face me, her hands in some kind of karate pose. I forced myself not to laugh as I stopped walking and stared at her.

"What the hell are you doing here?" she ground out.

"I'm here because my sister's freaking out."

She threw her arms in the air. "Why?"

"You seriously want me to answer that question?"

"No." She sighed, dragging her hands down her face.

"Why are you out here alone, Remington?"

"None of your business."

"Fair enough, but it *is* my sister's."

She nodded, crossing her arms and looking not only vulnerable as hell, but cold. After firing off a quick text to Grace to let her know Remington was safe, I stepped closer to Remington. "Baby—"

She waggled a finger at me. "No."

I walked toward her slowly and stopped when we were toe-to-toe. "What is going on with you, Rem? Huh? You shouldn't be out here alone in the dark. It's not safe."

"Puleeze, it's Vancouver, Washington. It's perfectly safe. I'm in more danger behind closed doors."

I frowned, sliding a hand to her neck and stroking her pulse. "What's going on?"

She shook her head.

Shrugging off my leather jacket, I wrapped it around her shoulders and pulled the front closed. "Need you to talk to me, Rem."

"What would be the point?"

"Oh, I don't know." I lifted her chin. "I might be able to help."

"My parents are insisting I go home."

"And what do you want?"

"I want to be a principal dancer in a respected ballet company…*not* in Savannah."

"So do that."

She rolled her eyes. "You make it all sound so easy."

"Isn't it?"

"Not really, no. They're holding my trust fund hostage until I do what they tell me to."

"Do you need your trust fund?"

"If I want a roof over my head, yes."

"Are you really standing here telling me you rely solely on trust fund money to survive?"

"If I was?" She wrinkled her nose and it was so fucking cute, it took an extensive amount of energy not to kiss her.

"Remi."

"Tweety," she mimicked.

"Why don't you come back to my place and we'll talk?"

"It's three in the morning."

"Got somewhere else you need to be?"

"*God,* why are you always such a pain in the ass?" she hissed.

"This ain't nothin', baby."

"That's what I'm afraid of," she grumbled.

* * *

Remington

Merrick chuckled, taking my hand and tugging me toward my car. At least I knew that once we were separated, I'd be able to ditch him. I just didn't really have anywhere to go…unless, I wanted to go back to my apartment. And I didn't. I was too afraid Vitaly might still be lurking.

As we approached my car, I noticed a young guy standing beside Merrick's truck and I couldn't stop myself from squeezing Merrick's hand and moving closer to him. He was right. It didn't matter that I was in suburbia, it wasn't safe to be out this late alone.

"It's all good, Rem. It's Cheese. He's gonna drive your car back to my place."

"Excuse me?"

"You heard me."

"I'm perfectly capable of driving."

"You're also perfectly capable of trying to ditch me and I'm not taking any chances."

"Pain in my ever-blessed ass."

He stopped walking and turned to face me. "Yeah, I heard that the first twelve times you said it. And you need to quit referencing your ass, Remi, because I've seen it. Up close and personal, and I liked what I saw. I still remember what your pussy tastes like, and I liked that too. But the thing I like most about you is your fuckin' sass, and since I also know your brain works faster than most, I'm not lettin' you figure out a way to slip through my fingers again. Got it?"

I bit my lip. God, I remember what it felt like when he tasted said pussy. He was a master with his tongue, and I'd been so rocked by him that night, I'd practically taken a vow of celibacy.

"Need you to acknowledge you hear me, Remington. Got it?"

I rolled my eyes. "Whatever."

"You got it." He made the statement and I glared at him.

"I don't have to 'get' shit, Merrick, you don't own me."

"We'll see about that." He took my hand again and walked us to our cars.

"Hey, brother," Cheese said as we approached.

"Did I wake you?" Merrick asked him.

"Nah. I was…," he glanced at me, then back at Merrick, "…entertaining. Had her drop me here."

Merrick smirked, then nodded at me. "Hand him your keys, Rem."

"No."

He faced me again and leaned down, so we were eye-to-eye. "Unless you want Cheese to rip the fuckin' dashboard apart and hotwire it, I'd suggest you hand him your keys."

I knew he was serious, and I was honestly too tired to argue with him, so I pulled my keys out of my pocket and handed them to Cheese.

"You're a dick," I snapped.

"Only if you're lucky," Merrick retorted and lifted me into his truck.

Without another word, he climbed in and we headed down the freeway.

By the time he pulled into the parking lot of what I assumed was his 'place,' I was pretty much ready to go full-on nuclear, and he would be the man to take the full brunt of my mushroom cloud. It was dark, so I had no idea where we were or what his condo building looked like on the outside. I just knew you had to have a code to get through the gate, so it felt safer than my apartment, and not just because Vitaly was out there somewhere.

Merrick climbed out of the truck and I saw him from the side mirror speaking with Cheese. I leaned over to the driver's seat to check and see if he might have left keys, but I was out of luck. I huffed just as my door was opened.

"Looking for a getaway option?" Merrick challenged.

I scowled at him but said nothing.

"Come on," he directed. "Let's go talk."

He helped me down and then we headed up to his condo. He entered another code to get into the building, then led me through a well-lit lobby area before stepping into an elevator and tugging me inside with him.

Traveling up to the seventh floor, we walked down a long hallway and stopped at the fifth door on the right. Unlocking his door, he pushed it open and stepped back so I could precede him inside.

He probably did that so I wouldn't run.

"Is Cheese coming to your place as well?" I asked.

"No. One of the other recruits is gonna pick him up."

"Why is Cheese called Cheese?" I asked.

"He doesn't stop smiling."

"Oh," I said, staring at my feet. I heard Merrick sigh and I looked up. "What?"

"Remington, you're safe here, you know that, right?"

"Not really, no."

"Will you tell me what the hell is going on? I know it's gotta be more than just your family situation."

"You don't want to know."

"I'm asking, Rem. I *do* want to know."

I have no idea why I broke. Chalk it up to exhaustion or my reactor melting down, but I decided if he wanted to know, he would know all of it. I pulled Merrick's jacket tighter around me and lowered myself to the sofa. "Do you know about the serial killer that was taunting Savannah? He just recently got killed."

"Thomas whatever the fuck?"

I nodded.

"Yeah. Alamo's a Dog."

"What's a dog?"

"Dogs of Fire. My club. Alamo's the Sergeant at Arms for our Savannah chapter and he's the one who killed the asshole."

"What?" I squeaked. "Why did he kill him?"

"Because the woman he took was Alamo's."

"Ohmigod," I breathed out, squeezing my eyes shut. "Jasmine was Alamo's girlfriend?"

"Now wife, yeah."

I nodded as I started to swallow convulsively. I knew Jasmine. Sort of. She was a year ahead of me in our private high school, and she'd always been nice, but we didn't quite move in the same circles.

"Who was he to you?" Merrick asked. "Thomas."

I bit my lip. "Technically…he was my ex-fiancé."

Merrick sat down and faced me. "Fuck."

"Don't get me wrong, I don't care that Thomas is dead. He was an awful human being. I just didn't realize you were that close to it."

"When were you supposed to get married?"

I shook my head. "We weren't getting married. I broke it off the day before I met you. It's why I was at the bar. My girls took me out to celebrate."

Merrick frowned. "And a woman went missing the next day."

I felt the sting of tears and nodded. "Yes."

"This isn't your fault."

"I know. I get it." I reached over and squeezed his hand. "Can you let me talk without commiserating or interrupting or doing your lawyer thing?"

"My lawyer thing?"

"Arguing."

"I'm not arguing."

I saw his slight smile and leaned back slightly. "Don't be a dick."

He raised his hands in surrender. "I will cease and desist being a dick immediately."

"Thank you." I burrowed deeper into Merrick's jacket, letting its warmth seep into me. "Thomas was insane, obviously, but he's old money and my parents wanted an advantageous union. I was the sacrificial lamb. Of course, I didn't know any of this until a week before I broke off the engagement. All I knew was that a handsome, rich, and sweet man was showing me affection that seemed genuine. That all lasted a year."

Merrick rose to his feet. "Keep talking, I'm gonna grab a beer. Want anything?"

I shook my head. Merrick stepped around his island and

opened the fridge while I tried to figure out how to info dump everything.

"Just spit it out, Rem," Merrick said, taking his seat again.

"I don't even know why I'm telling you all of this, to be honest."

"Because I'm a good listener."

"You think so?"

"I know so." He tipped his beer toward me. "Keep going."

"We'd been dating for about a year or so when Thomas proposed. I was over the moon happy…as were my parents. I'd made an extremely advantageous match and I was in love. Win-win." I bit my lip, my memories flooding back to Savannah. "It all changed after we were engaged. He started getting weird sexually."

"Weird how?"

"I really don't think you want to know. Let's just say it surpassed Christian Grey kinky and went into psychopathic deviance."

"Shit."

"Yeah. He spent several months trying to cajole me into all manner of grossness, and he'd call me frigid if I didn't. All the typical abuser stuff. I mean, for the love of God, I was not going to let that man shove his feet into my pussy."

"Are you fucking serious?" he hissed.

"As a heart attack. I recognized it for what it was and broke up with him, making sure we were in a public place and handing him my engagement ring. Three days later, he broke into my apartment."

"Did he steal shit?"

I shook my head.

He studied me. "Were you home?"

I nodded, picking at invisible lint on my leg.

"Babe?"

I looked up at him. "What?"

"What happened?"

I shook my head again.

"Did he…hurt you?"

I nodded, swallowing convulsively before taking a deep breath. I needed to say the words out loud, even if it felt impossible. "He raped me."

"Fuck, baby, I'm sorry."

The anger pouring off Merrick was palpable, but in a weird way, it made me feel safe, because I knew it wasn't directed at me, but *for* me. "I reported him. Went to the hospital, everything they tell you you're supposed to do, and his family buried it."

The vein on Merrick's neck began to pulse and he turned his head away from me.

"I think I should stop."

He shook his head. "No. Don't. Tell me all of it."

Surprisingly, I didn't want to stop. I wanted to tell him everything…I wouldn't, but I wanted to. I trusted him. I always had. It was probably why I slept with him in the first place.

"When I told my parents what Thomas had done, they said I must have led him on somehow. Gave him mixed messages." I blinked back tears. "I sat in their formal living room, my face beat to shit, and they said I led him on. Then they had the audacity to tell me I should ask for his forgiveness and try to get the engagement back on. Well, my mother did, anyway. Daddy had a client meeting."

"Fuck your parents."

"Oh, believe me, I would. But they froze my accounts and I had nothing."

"They can't legally do that."

I sighed. "Merrick, I know that, but they did. I don't know how, but they did. Daddy's a lawyer—"

His eyes widened. "So *this* is why you hate lawyers."

"Yes. Sorry, Tweety."

"Only a little offense taken."

I smiled. "My name is mud in Savannah, so I haven't been able to find someone to help me figure it out. My family has reach, the likes of which you've never seen."

"Can I ask something that might be hard to answer?"

"Sure."

"Why'd you sleep with me, if you'd endured a rape?"

I studied him a second. "I didn't. I slept with you the night after I broke off the engagement. He raped me after."

"Fuck me, seriously?"

I nodded.

"Did he know about our night?"

I stared at my hands.

"Remington."

"Merrick, don't."

"Goddammit!" He knifed off the sofa, dragging his hands through his hair and pacing the room. "I shoulda been more aware."

"How?" I challenged.

"He was obviously stalking you, Remington. I should have been more on guard."

"Oh my god, Merrick. You knew me for three hours, he'd known me for four years. He was also a sociopathic murderer, so will you please stow your guilt? There was nothing either of us could have done at that point."

What he didn't realize, was that I'd called back memories of our night together in the midst of the worst of Thomas's attack. I really believe it's what saved me.

I planned to keep that nugget of information from him, however.

"Did you get help after? See someone?" he asked, gently.

"Yes. I drove to Brighton once a week. It was a way to keep it private."

Truth be told, it took me almost three months to find a therapist who was removed from Savannah society. Until then, I'd had to stow my feelings deep down inside.

"Baby, I'm so sorry you had to deal with all that shit," he said, sitting down again. "I wish you'd called me, but I understand why you didn't."

"The really shitty part of all of it was that, at first, I didn't realize Thomas was alienating me from my friends. Classic abuser behavior and I didn't recognize it until I got away. I was pissed at myself because I was so aware of shit like that. As soon as red flags popped up, I called Thomas on it and watched. He was on his best behavior for a long time, but by then, I had only two true friends left. Chel and Kennedy. They were actually the ones who encouraged me to leave Savannah." I drew my knees up to my chest and settled my chin on them. "I wish I'd done it earlier, to be honest."

"Hindsight's twenty-twenty, though, Rem. Give yourself a break."

"Yeah."

"Why'd you sneak out of Flea's place?"

I shrugged. "I felt like the walls were closing in on me. I just needed air."

"How about now?"

"I'm good."

"Look at me when you lie to me."

"I'm good, Tweety." I met his eyes and smiled. "At the risk of making your head bigger, right now's the first time I've felt safe in months."

"I fucking hate you've had to deal with that shit, but glad you feel good now."

"Do you have any ibuprofen?"

His eyebrows drew together. "You in pain?"

"Just a headache."

He headed into the kitchen returning with a bottled water and handed me the ibuprofen. I doled out four and took them, setting the water on the coffee table. "Thanks."

He held his hands out and smiled. "Come on. You're

gonna soak, then you're going to bed."

"Soak?"

"You'll see."

I took his hand and let him pull me up off the sofa, then followed him down the hallway and into his bedroom. I stalled. "Merrick, this isn't what I had in mind."

He chuckled, closing the distance between us and wrapping an arm around my waist. "Ignore the mess."

He pushed me forward, through another door and into one of the nicest bathrooms I'd ever seen…and believe me, I'd know…my aunt had one made out of gold. Ostentatious and not at all my style, it had cost almost a million dollars…a mere drop in the bucket for my aunt and uncle.

Merrick's bathroom had a huge claw-foot tub, a shower big enough for four with eight shower heads, and a huge counter with two sinks, plus plenty of storage. Everything was done in marble and it didn't fit his biker style. At. All. It was stunning.

"Wow," I whispered.

He grinned. "Grace made me buy the place because of this bathroom. And, not that I let my sister's opinion sway me, the bathroom is pretty spectacular."

"It really is," I agreed.

"Start the tub. I'll see if Grace left any of her shit here. I doubt you want to use my Old Spice body wash."

I nodded, and he went off to find Grace's "shit."

THREE

Finch

AFTER FINDING SOME of Grace's body wash and girly shampoo shit, I left Remington to relax and headed back to the kitchen for my phone. I dialed my sister.

"Is she okay?" Grace asked.

"Yeah, sissy. She's here and she's safe."

"But is she okay?"

"She's getting there."

"What happened?"

"Not my story to tell, Gracie."

She huffed. "Fine. Be a gentleman."

"You wanna bring her bag over here for me in the morning?"

"Why?"

I grabbed another beer and popped the top. "Because

she's staying here until this shit's sorted."

"Is she okay with that?"

"She will be."

Grace sighed. "I'm going to ask her myself."

"Go ahead."

"And if she gives me a different story—"

"She's still gonna stay here," I said and took a swig of beer.

"Merrick."

"You gonna bring her bag by tomorrow?"

"*If* she wants to stay, yes."

"Okay, sissy, I'll swing by and pick it up then."

"Oh my god, Merrick, you're being insane."

"I'm gonna let you go, Grace."

"Don't force her to do something she doesn't want to do."

This pissed me off and I scowled as I ground out, "Grace, have I ever forced anyone to do something they didn't want to do?"

"Well, no, but you seem a little off-kilter when it comes to Remington, so I'm saying it out loud, in case."

"Got it. Gonna hang up now."

"I love you, big brother."

"Love you too, Gracie. Conditionally."

She giggled and hung up, then I fired off a text to Flea. I'd let him deal with my sister. I headed into my guest bedroom and stripped the bed.

My sister had been staying with me while she figured out what to do with her life after college, but since our grandmother had hurt herself, Grace was staying with her in the interim. Although, Flick seemed to be relishing the job, so it was more accurate to assume Grace would be at Flea's more often than not.

I probably should have changed the sheets earlier, but I didn't really have any plans for anyone to visit other than my sister. Now, I hoped Remington would stay for as long as she needed to feel safe, so I domesticated-up and made the bed.

I saw that Grace had left a robe hanging in her closet, so I grabbed it and made my way to my bedroom, pushing open the door and calling out, "Rem, I have a robe for you. I'll leave it on my bed."

"Thanks, Tweety."

I fucking loved how she called me Tweety. I'd never let *her* know that, but it was cute as hell and I noticed she only used it when she felt comfortable. Even if she was comfortable and pissed at me.

I headed back to the living room and settled onto the sofa. It was almost four in the morning, but I didn't have a heavy case load at the moment, so I could take a day to make sure Remi was good, and maybe catch up on some sleep.

"Hey," Remi said quietly, and I craned my neck to look at her.

"Hey. You good?"

She smiled. "I'm so good. That bath is amazing."

I grinned. "I told you."

She made her way to the sofa and sat facing me. "Thanks, Merrick."

"You're welcome."

"So…are you okay if I stay here tonight? Well, this morning as the case may be."

"You can stay here as long as you want," I said. "I changed the sheets in the guest room."

She raised an eyebrow. "You changed the sheets?"

"I do have *some* knowledge of domestic shit."

"Apparently."

"You have to promise me something," I said.

"What?"

"No running off in the middle of the night. If you want to leave, you're free to go, but just let me know first, okay?"

"Like, really free to go?"

"You're not a prisoner, Rem."

"But if I said to you, 'Tweety, I'm gonna go to XYZ,' you'd just let me go?"

"Of course I would."

I narrowed my eyes. "Tweety."

He sighed. "I'm not saying you wouldn't have a recruit on you, or I wouldn't be tracking your phone…"

"Aha!" I exclaimed, pointing a finger at him. "I knew it."

"Want you safe, Rem. That's all."

"Promise?"

"Promise."

"Okay, Tweety. I can give that to you."

I nodded. "I appreciate that. Come on, I'll show you where everything is."

* * *

Remington

I followed Merrick down the hall and into what was obviously Grace's room. In fact, some of her things were still there.

"I'm sure Grace won't mind if you borrow something of hers, but if you need anything specific, let me know."

"A T-shirt would be appreciated," I said. "Grace is quite a bit smaller than me."

That was somewhat of an understatement. I was almost an E-cup in the boob department and had to wear both a minimizing bra and a chest binding contraption on dance nights in order to stay balanced. It was an ordeal, but one that I endured gladly, because ballet was my life.

He smiled. "I'll grab you one of mine."

Merrick returned within minutes with one of his black club tees. I took it from him and smiled. "Thanks."

Giving me space, he leaned against the doorframe.

"You okay?"

I bit my lip. "Honestly?"

"Always."

"I feel safe."

His eyes got soft and he smiled. "I like that, Remi."

"When's Grace coming back?"

"Not for a while. You can stay here as long as you need to."

"I should go back to my place tomorrow. I can't hide forever."

"How about you stay here until Vitaly's dealt with?"

I tried to hide my elation. "You wouldn't mind?"

"Fuck, Rem." He frowned. "Just how freaked are you?"

"Freaked," I whispered.

"Really wanna touch you right now." He held a hand out. "You okay with that?"

I blinked back tears and walked into his arms. He held me gently and stroked my back as I burrowed into his chest.

"I'm really sorry I didn't call you back."

He gave me a gentle squeeze. "I'm working on forgiving you for that."

I gasped and glanced up at him. "It was a one-night—" I saw his smile and cut off my admonishment, wrinkling my nose to cover a smile and burrowing back into his chest. "You're an ass."

Merrick chuckled. "Got you to smile, though."

"Whatever."

The sound of his doorbell interrupted our moment and Merrick stiffened. "Close the door and don't open it until I come and get you."

My heart raced. "Why?"

He reached for my doorknob. "Just do it."

I leaned against the door and waited.

And waited.

I heard low voices and cracked the door slightly to listen better.

"I want to see Remi," Grace demanded, and I smiled.

Lordy, she and her brother were cut from the same cloth. I opened the door more and walked out to the front room.

"I'm here," I said, and Grace made a dash for me. "I'm so sorry I didn't tell you I was leaving."

"We'll talk about that later…when I can verbally spank you," Grace threatened.

"Can't wait." I smiled. "What are you doing here?"

"Merrick thought you might like some of your things, so I brought your bag."

Well, that was seriously sweet. I avoided looking at him, lest I swoon and ask to suck his cock, and focused on Grace. "Thanks. I didn't think I could bring myself to borrow a pair of your undies."

She rolled her eyes. "Well, you could have…but you would have had to keep them."

"Fair enough."

"Are you okay, honey?" she asked. "You're welcome to come back with me and Flea."

I covertly glanced at Merrick, but he was in a conversation with Flea in the kitchen, so I relaxed. "No, I'm okay here. I really am sorry I ran out. I just felt overwhelmed."

"I absolutely understand that emotion." Grace squeezed my arm. "If you're sure you're okay, I'll take Flea home and do unspeakable things to him."

"I heard that," Flea called.

"I was hoping you did."

I chuckled. "Go. I'm really okay."

"Don't have to tell me twice," Flea said, already moving toward us.

Grace hugged me and then she and Flea left without any fanfare.

Merrick grabbed my bag and carried it back to the room and I followed.

"I'm gonna get some sleep," he said. "You should too."

"Okay, Merr. Thanks."

"If you need me, you come get me."

"I won't need you."

He seemed disappointed by that, but quickly covered his expression with a smile. "I'll see you when I wake up."

"Okay, Tweety. Thanks."

He stroked my cheek gently, then headed to his room, while I closed my door and dressed for bed…keeping his T-shirt on.

* * *

The smell of coffee wafted into my room and I couldn't keep my eyes closed. I also smelled bacon. I had been crash-dieting ever since I started my internship with PBC, so bacon had been off the table…but now, mmm…bacon.

I sat up. I could eat whatever the hell I wanted to right now.

And I wanted bacon.

I slipped down the hall into the guest bathroom and cleaned up a little, then headed to the kitchen. Merrick's back was to me, so I took a second to watch him. Broad shoulders, perfectly sculpted ass sat atop long, muscular legs showcased by his dark jeans, and I just wanted to run my hands over every inch. Lordy, he was pretty from behind.

"Coffee's in the pot."

"How did you know it was me?" I asked.

He grinned over his shoulder. "Who else would it be?"

"I mean, how did you hear me with all that frying going on?"

He turned to face me, sliding bacon onto a plate. "The bathroom door squeaks."

I stared at the bacon. "I noticed that."

"You hungry?"

"Starving," I said, still staring at the bacon.

Merrick chuckled. "Help yourself."

I snagged a piece off the plate and bit into it. "Oh my god, bacon, I've missed you."

"You want eggs?"

"I would love eggs. But, first, coffee."

He nodded to his right. "In the pot," he repeated. "Mugs are left of the sink. Cream is in the fridge, sugar in the cannister to the left of the pot."

I found everything I needed and made a cup of coffee, freshening his, then sitting at the island.

Merrick's phone buzzed on the counter and he leaned down to look at the screen before picking it up. "Hey, Hatch." He nodded and glanced at me. "Yeah. No shit? Yeah, give me an hour. Thanks." He hung up and leaned across the counter toward me. "Hatch found Vitaly."

I gasped, setting my fork down. "Is he in custody?"

"No."

"What? Why not?"

"Not how we do things."

"Who?"

He grinned, straightening and serving up the scrambled eggs.

"Are you going to answer my question?" I pressed.

"No," he said.

"Why not?"

"Because we're gonna take care of him in our own way, and it's better you don't know the details."

"Where is he?" I asked.

"Somewhere secure."

I frowned. "Which is *where*?"

He grinned, turning off the stove. "I gotta head out."

"Tweety—"

"I'll leave you a key."

I let out a frustrated squeak…just as my phone pealed. I snagged it from where it was charging and saw Grace was calling. "Hi Grace."

"What's wrong?"

I sighed. "Just how close are you to your brother?"

"Why, what did he do?"

"Answer the question first."

"He's my second favorite person."

"Shit," I hissed. "So, if I murdered him, you'd miss him."

She laughed. "A little bit, yes."

"Well, damn."

"Feel like hitting a dance class with me?"

"Yes," I answered immediately.

"Okay, I'll pick you up in twenty minutes. Cassidy said she'll hold two spots for us."

"That sounds great," I said, and we hung up. I cleaned up and loaded the dishwasher, then went to gather my dance things, running into Merrick in the hallway.

"Heading out?" he asked.

"Grace is picking me up for a class." I raised an eyebrow. "But I'm guessing you already knew that."

He smiled. "Maybe."

"Where are you going?"

"Out."

I narrowed my eyes. "I *will* find out, Tweety."

"You think?"

I let out a quiet grunt and Merrick laughed.

"Pain in my ass," I hissed.

He stopped laughing and I realized it was probably because he was thinking about my ass. Shit. I was kind of thinking about his now, too.

"Um…can I go back to my place since you have Vitaly…um, where again?"

"You are free to move about the cabin," Merrick said. "But you're also welcome to stay here a little while longer as well."

"I should go home."

"Okay, baby. Leave your stuff and I'll drop it by when

I'm done."

"Where are you going?"

He grinned. "Nice try."

I rolled my eyes just as Grace called out, "I'm here."

I wagged a finger at him. "Your sister saved you this time, Big Bird."

"You feel free to keep your illusions, princess."

"I'm no princess, Tweety."

"No?"

"I'm the fuckin' queen."

He laughed again and shook his head as he led me out to the front room.

"Okay, so you've kissed and made up," Grace said.

"What do you mean?" Merrick asked, grabbing his keys.

"Nothing," I rushed to say, giving Grace a warning glare.

"I'm gonna head out," he said, and hugged his sister. "Have fun." He didn't hug me, but he did give me a gentle smile that sent shock waves to my nether regions.

Jebus, this man is going to kill me.

"Ready?" Grace asked.

"Yep. I'll follow you."

"I'll drive. I can drop you back here."

I shook my head. "I'm going home after."

"Did Merr say that was okay?" she asked.

I frowned. "Are you high?"

"What?"

"Merrick has no say over what I do and don't do."

She stared at me like I was an alien. "Remi. Seriously."

I sighed. "He said I was safe to go home."

She relaxed. "Okay, good."

"Where would they take Vitaly?"

Grace shrugged. "No clue."

"Are you under a gag order?"

She chuckled. "No, I really don't know. They have a

super-secret lair where they take their enemies.”

“Shit.”

“Come on. You need to stretch your muscles. I hope you’re ready to die.”

“Bring it on,” I said, and followed her out of Merrick’s place.

FOUR

Finch

I PARKED MY truck in the rear lot of Blush and headed down the concrete stairwell that led to the club's basement. I motioned to the surveillance camera mounted overhead and was immediately buzzed in. The club's basement was sometimes referred to as the "Woodshed," as it was here that lessons that could only be learned with a switch were dispensed. As I entered the space, I could see Hatch and Flea standing on either side of Vitaly, who was gagged and zip-tied to a metal folding chair.

"You asked to be looped in, so we waited for you," Hatch said matter-of-factly.

"I appreciate it," I said with a casual nod, the door closing behind me.

The basement was mostly empty except for some plumbing materials leaning in the corner, opposite the doorway, but I knew they wouldn't be stored there for very long. Mack and Booker ran the club, and every area was highly organized…everything had a place, which was not in the corner of the basement.

Hatch pulled me in close and nodded toward Vitaly. "The only reason you're here is because I know Remington is tight with you and your sister," he said. "Flea's assured me that you won't get carried away, and I'm counting on the fact that you know how to keep your mouth shut."

"Yeah, man," I said.

"Good, because you know we don't like gettin' our hands dirty, but sometimes you have to take out the fucking trash before it starts stinkin' up the place," he said looking over at Vitaly, who sat motionless, eyes straight ahead. "This guy's family back in Russia is loaded, so bribin' him isn't going to be an option. Wailin' on him didn't seem to do the trick, so I'm gonna have one more go at scarin' the little prick out of town, then we'll have to improvise." Hatch walked over to Vitaly, leaned in close to him and said, "I'm gonna take this gag out of your mouth, and if you scream I'll hit you so hard, you'll lose the will to ever utter a sound again." Vitaly remained still and Hatch untied his gag. "It appears that I didn't make myself clear the last time I had my *little chat* with you."

"Such a conversationalist you are," Vitaly said. "You broke two of my ribs."

"And, yet, here we are once again," Hatch said. "I told you to stay away from Remington Charles, and what did you do? If a few body shots didn't get the point across last time, perhaps it's time to mess up that pretty-boy face of yours."

"Why the fuck do you macho assholes care so much about one bitch anyway?" Vitaly asked.

"She's a friend of ours, and we protect our friends," I snapped. "But, I'm sure you wouldn't know anything about that, you fucking sociopath."

"What do you know about me?" Vitaly asked defiantly. "I understand loyalty more than you could ever know," he said with a sneer. "I'm also wise enough not to waste my loyalty on whores."

I moved toward Vitaly, but Hatch stepped between us.

"A word of advice," Hatch said. "You might want to watch how you talk about women when you're around us. Next time, I ain't stopping him."

"Women deserve respect, I agree," Vitaly said. "But these girls aren't real women. They are merely dancers."

"What the fuck are you talking about?" I asked. "You're a dancer."

"I'm not a fucking *dancer*. I'm an artist and a businessman," he said smugly.

"I apologize, Lord Twinkletoes, I didn't realize we were in the presence of such artistic greatness," Hatch said with an exaggerated bow.

"You are," Vitaly said plainly. "I excel at what I do, and you are lucky to have me in your country. Rich Americans pay me to come here and dance for them and they are right to do so. My uncles are lucky because while I'm here, I can help them find new talent for their clubs," he said with an evil grin.

My shoulders stiffened, and my hands balled up into tight fists.

"It's true," Vitaly continued. "Every one of those girls thinks they are going to be the next prima ballerina, but I'm there to show them just how mediocre they all are."

"I've heard enough from this narcissistic piece of shit. Let's just beat the shit out of him and be done with it," I said, my anger level rising.

"Hold on," Hatch said, pulling me to the side. "We're not here to torture him, we're here to make sure he leaves Remington and the rest of the dancers alone."

"What? It was okay for you and Flea to have a go at him, but now we're above that?" I challenged.

"Beating him up didn't stop him last time. We need to figure out what it's gonna take to make this guy leave town, without drawing any heat on the club."

"It's rude to whisper about someone when they are in the room," Vitaly said.

"Okay, asshole," I said turning to face him. "How about this? Leave Remington alone, and leave the conservatory for good, or we'll make the last beating look like a hug."

Vitaly laughed loudly. "You guys talk so fucking macho. Just like my uncles. Look, I get it. You have a hard-on for Remington, and you want me to stay away from her. Fine, but just make sure that she knows that when she's three months behind on rent, my family is more than happy to give her employment suitable to her skillset."

I threw a wild right hook and connected squarely with the left side of Vitaly's skull, causing my middle knuckle to feel like it broke on impact.

"I warned you," Hatch said to Vitaly, as blood began to pour from the gash in the side of his head.

I did my best to hide the throbbing pain in my right hand before returning my attention back to a dazed Vitaly. "You wanna say something like that again, you rapist piece of shit?"

"Rapist?" Vitaly said, as his eyes began to refocus. "I've never raped anyone. I can have any woman I want, any time I want."

"Not if we let him keep goin' at your face like that," Flea chimed in.

"Remington said you attacked her, and I believe her. If you didn't get the message before, you're gonna get it now, you son of a bitch," I said, loading up my rapidly swelling right hand.

"Easy, Finch," Hatch said. "Let's avoid too many head shots. I think Vitaly's got the point that we're serious. Don't you Vitaly?"

He nodded, blood streaming down his neck.

"Good. Because we want you on the first available flight to Moscow."

"Bullshit," Vitaly spit out.

"You're either going to the airport in the morning, or to the cops to admit what you did to Remington," Hatch said in a tone that was void of negotiation.

"I'm not leaving the United States! You will never get away with this. I am guest in your country. I am here to share my talents as the premier ballet dancer of Russia, and I will not be intimidated. Your government has assured my safety as an ambassador."

"You feel safe right now?" Flea asked.

"What are you going to do? Kill me? I don't think so. Too much "heat" as you say. You want to keep beating me up? That will look pretty suspicious to the authorities wouldn't you say?"

"He's right," I said. "It's his word against Remi's, and his family is too connected within the dance world for them to ever side with her. Cut him loose."

"What the fuck?" Hatch asked.

"What can we do? As long as he's in the US as a sponsored artist, he's too high-profile for us to be fucking with. The club's safety has to come first. Remi's career with the Conservatory is over anyway, and the cops don't believe her, so just let him go."

Hatch looked stunned, as did Vitaly. "Finch, I don't know what the fuck you're think—"

"Goddammit, Hatch, just cut him loose."

Hatch looked at me with fire in his eyes but trusted me enough to cut Vitaly's restraints. Once they were cut, Vitaly quickly rose to his feet, and put his hand to his head wound. "You're gonna pay for this," he said.

"Just get the fuck out," I said, backing up.

Vitaly smirked and slowly walked toward the door which he'd almost reached before I smashed his knee with a three-foot piece of galvanized pipe I'd grabbed from the corner. I felt his leg snap in two like a chicken bone, and Vitaly dropped to the ground like a stone.

"Oh, shit," I said. "That sounded like a career-ending injury to me. Did you guys hear that?"

"Jesus, Finch. What the fuck did you just do?" Hatch asked.

"You said not to hit him in the face," I replied.

"How the fuck is this not going to bring attention on us?" Hatch yelled.

"You said we needed to give him a reason to go back to Moscow. Well, here it is. If he can't dance, then he has no fucking reason to be here. Problem solved."

"Hey, this guy's goin' into shock," Flea called out.

"Fuck him," I said, taken aback by my own words, not to mention my actions. However, something inside of me snapped when he'd called Remington a whore and threatened her. I knew as long as this guy had a reason to be around her, he'd use it to his advantage, so I had to make sure he'd never dance again.

"I'm callin' Katie," Flea said.

I rolled my eyes. Katie was Flea's sister and a registered nurse. The amount of folks she'd stitched up on the downlow was probably in the hundreds by now, which is why we called her. She was discreet and genuinely cared about every one of us…and she was the last person I wanted 'treating' Vitaly. "Leave the piece of shit to rot."

Hatch approached me slowly. Like a lion tamer approaching an out of control cat. "Finch."

"What?" I seethed as I stared at Vitaly, now passed out on the ground.

"Brother."

"What?"

"Merrick, look at me."

I turned my focus onto Hatch and he raised an eyebrow.

"What?" I repeated.

He settled his hands on my shoulders and shook his

head. "You got somethin' you need to tell me?"

"Like?"

"Like, why you're freakin' over a woman you don't know."

"I know her."

"Yeah, I'm pickin' up on that." He patted my shoulders as he sighed. "You need to get gone. We'll clean this up."

"Don't really feel finished."

"As your superior, I'm tellin' you that you are."

"Technically—"

"You get the fuck outta here or you and I are gonna have a conversation that you will find painful. Don't make me deal with you in an official capacity, pup. You and your shiny new patch won't like it."

I bit back a retort. It would land on deaf ears, and since Hatch was an officer of my club, he had seniority. Plus, he was like my second dad. I respected him, and it wasn't him I had a beef with. So, I lowered my head and stepped back.

Flea closed the distance between us. "You got time to pick Grace up from class?" He nodded over his shoulder. "Gonna be a while."

"Didn't she drive?"

"She did, but I had Cheese pick her car up, so I could drive her home."

Made sense. Flea was overprotective like that. "Yeah, brother," I said.

"Thanks, man."

I nodded and headed to my truck. When I'd left my condo earlier, it had been too wet to ride, so I'd taken my pickup, but now it was sunny and dry, and I cursed the Portland weather.

Fuck, I wanted to ride.

FIVE

Remington

LOWERED MYSELF to the floor when Cassidy ended the class, dragging my legs in front of me and leaning over them to grip my ankles as I tried to stretch my muscles back into some form of shape. Good God, the woman was a masochist.

Grace flopped down beside me and mirrored my pose. "I hate her."

I grinned. "Me too."

"She's awesome, huh?"

"Incredible," I agreed.

As I pulled my toe shoes off, Grace pulled her phone out of her bag and put it to her ear, drawing my attention when she gasped. Her eyes flew to me and she lowered her phone slowly. "Ohmigod."

"What?"

Leaning closer, she whispered, "My brother broke Vitaly's kneecap."

"What?" I squeaked.

"He will never dance again."

"Seriously?"

She nodded.

"Excuse me," I said, and rose to my feet, blinking back tears as I walked quickly toward the bathroom.

"Remi!" a deep voice called, and I turned to find Merrick following me. "You okay?"

I didn't answer him, just took a flying leap toward him. He caught me, and I wrapped myself around him and sobbed into his chest.

"Fuck, baby, what happened?"

I shook my head, burrowing deeper.

"Rem, you're scaring me, honey. What the hell happened?"

"You…broke…his…kneecap."

His body stiffened. "Who told you that?"

"Grace," I said on a hiccup.

He relaxed and gave me a gentle squeeze. "Are you coming back to my place?"

I shook my head again.

"I'm going to you, then?"

I nodded and got another squeeze.

"Gotta drop Grace home, then I'll be by."

"Okay," I sniffed holding him tighter so he wouldn't let me go.

"But I got a minute to stand here if you need me to."

I nodded into his chest again and Merrick chuckled, pulling me closer.

"Okay, honey, I got you."

His hand went to the back of my neck and he stroked gently while I held him tightly and we stood in the middle of the hallway as dancers milled around us. I was surprised no one bothered us, but chalked it up to Merrick wearing his badass biker uniform. Sexy as hell, but also extremely intimidating.

"Okay, I'm done waiting," Grace said, and pulled me away from Merrick. "What happened?"

"Nothing, Grace. I'm okay. I think I'm just really tired."

She frowned at her brother. "What did you say to her?"

He raised his hands in surrender and I sighed. "Seriously, honey, I'm fine. I'm exhausted and I had a mini-meltdown. It's all good now."

"I think you should come home with me."

"No," I said immediately. "I want to sleep in my own bed. I promise, if that changes, I'll let you know."

She narrowed her eyes, but finally gave me a nod. "Even if it's the middle of the night."

I smiled. "Even if it's the middle of the night."

"Grab your stuff, Grace," Merrick said. "We'll walk Remi to her car."

I followed Grace back into the room, pulled on sweats and my tennis shoes, then we headed out to the cars.

Merrick waited for me to climb in and start my car before heading to his truck. He then followed me until he had to split off to take Grace to Flea's.

I drove to my apartment and let myself in, feeling safe for the first time in a long time. I showered, then dressed in a pair of sweats and a tank top. It was unusually warm and I kind of wished I had sprung for the air-conditioning unit. It was another fifty bucks a month, though, and I just couldn't justify the expense.

I dragged my box fan out of the closet and pointed it toward the sofa before flopping down and trying to find something on TV, just as my phone rang. "Hey, Poohbah."

Michelle Colter and I used to work together at our local coffee house in Savannah when we were teens. She was actually my manager, and we all used to call her the 'Grand Poohbah,' because when I first met her, I thought she was bossy. What I pretty quickly discovered, was she was brutally honest and defended her friends to the death. 'Poohbah' stuck, though, and Kennedy had also adopted the nickname.

"Are you sitting down?" she asked.

"Yes. What's wrong?"

She was fighting Leukemia…had been for over ten years. She'd been misdiagnosed for six years until they finally figured it out and it had been nothing but a nightmare.

"I talked to the doctor today."

I sat up, my heart racing. "And, it's bad?"

"He gave me less than six months."

"What? I thought the chemo was working."

She sighed. "I stopped chemo."

"When?"

"Three weeks ago."

"Chel, you can't just give up."

"I'm not giving up, honey. The chemo wasn't working. It was killing me faster than the cancer."

I swiped the tears from my cheeks. "There has to be something more they can do. You can't stop fighting."

"I'm not," she said with a sad chuckle. "They're working on it. There's an experimental treatment, but I'm not sure I'm going to qualify."

"What now?"

"We wait, honey."

I muted my phone, so she wouldn't hear my sobs.

"But, enough about me," Michelle said. "How's PBC?"

"I was fired."

"What?" she exclaimed.

I sighed, then filled her in on everything that had happened over the last week.

"Holy shit, Remi. What is up with all these assholes who like to use you as a punching bag?"

"I don't know. I'm over it, though."

"Yeah. I can't believe that hottie from the bar's your

friend's brother, though."

"Right? I probably should have asked more questions when we hooked up, but I was too busy experiencing orgasm after orgasm."

Michelle groaned. "Way too much information, Remington."

"I know." I smiled. "I could have asked him in between, but that was when I had his cock in my mouth, so…"

"Oh my god, bitch, stop." My friend dissolved into laughter and my heart felt a little lighter than it had a few minutes ago.

"He did this thing with his tongue—"

"I'm hanging up on you now," she threatened.

"Okay, I'll stop." I chuckled.

"I promise, I'll let you know if the end is nigh."

"Dramatic to the end, I see."

She chuckled. "Just wait until you see what's on my tombstone."

"I thought you were donating your body to science."

"Oh, I am, but I still want a tombstone."

I rolled my eyes. "Okay, Pooh, we'll get you a tombstone. But not for at least twenty years, so you can't die until then."

"Workin' on it, buddy."

"I appreciate that."

"I need to get to bed. I'll call you next week."

"Sounds good," I said. "Love you, Chel."

"Love you, too, honey."

We hung up and the stress of the past week swamped me as I curled into the fetal position on the sofa and cried.

* * *

Banging forced its way into my brain and I rubbed my gritty eyes. It sounded like the building was coming down. "Remington Charles, open this fucking door!"

I jumped off the sofa with a squeak.

"Remington!"

I rushed to my door and called out, "Merrick?"

"Open the door," he demanded.

I checked the peephole, then pulled open the door. "Why are you yelling? My neighbors are gonna get pissed."

He pushed in, closing and locking it behind him. "I've been knocking and ringing the doorbell for almost five minutes. What the fuck?"

"I must have fallen asleep," I explained, biting back a yawn. "Sorry."

He relaxed, but still pulled me in for a hug. "Fuck, Rem. You scared the shit out of me."

I fisted my hands at my sides. I didn't want to 'scare the shit' out of him. I didn't want him to care that much. "I really am sorry, but I think maybe I should just go to bed. You and I can talk another day, okay?"

"Hey." He frowned, lifting my chin. "You're safe. Vitaly's on his way back to Russia. He apparently raped the daughter of a high-level official, so he's gonna be dealt with in the mother land."

"Really?"

"Yes."

"He's gone?"

"Pretty sure he's already left the country," Merrick said.

I dropped my head with a nod.

"Did I do this?"

"Do what?" I asked the floor.

"Make you shrink away all of a sudden?"

I squeezed my eyes shut. "You don't have that kind of power."

"Fuck," he whispered. "Honey, come here."

"I'm here."

"Look at me."

I swallowed and raised my head, forcing myself not to break. "Tweety, stop."

"Stop what?"

"Looking at me like that."

He smiled. "Can't help the way I look, Rem."

I rolled my eyes, the action causing a tear to escape.

Merrick wiped it away gently with his thumb. "So fucking beautiful."

"Don't."

"Don't what?"

"Don't be sweet."

He grinned. "Okay, Rem, I'll stop immediately."

"Good."

His hand slid to my neck and he raised my chin again. "You're safe."

"For now."

"For always, Rem."

"Am I safe from you?" I whispered.

He frowned, his gaze pensive. "Are you afraid of me?"

Such a loaded question. I was afraid he'd disappear on me. I was afraid I'd do something reprehensible, and he'd never speak to me again. The fear was physical, and I rubbed my chest. "Only in here."

Merrick touched his mouth to mine gently, before kissing one cheek, then the other and wrapping his arms around me. "I've got you."

"You shouldn't."

"Why not?"

I squeezed my eyes shut as I confessed, "Because I might seem strong on the outside, but I'm really damaged goods."

Despite my self-imposed darkness, I felt his body stiffen. "Last time."

I met his eyes. "What?"

"If I ever hear you say anything like that about yourself again, I'm gonna fuckin' tear down the walls around us."

I pressed my lips into a thin line…not from fear, but to keep myself from laughing.

"You think that's funny?" he challenged, and I lost my battle with mirth, gripping his arms and laughing until I almost cried.

"God damn, you're fuckin' cute when you're crazy."

"You think I'm crazy?" I asked.

"You wanna explain the laughing?"

"So serious, Big Bird," I teased, biting back another laugh.

Before I could make another retort, his lips were on mine and I found myself gripping his vest to stay upright. God, he tasted amazing. Like mint.

"Fuck!" he hissed after breaking the kiss and stepping away. "I'm sorry, Remi."

"Don't," I rasped, reaching for him. "Don't stop."

"I have to."

"Why?"

He shook his head. "With you looking at me like that, I honestly have no idea."

I licked my lips. "Stay."

"Remi, I stay, and this happens, we're in this. I won't make another one-night stand agreement with you. I want more."

"Oh," I whispered.

He stepped further back and crossed his arms. "Yeah, Remi. 'Oh.'"

"I thought bikers were whores."

A shadow of a smile crossed his lips. "Yeah? Who'd you hear that from?"

"Everyone."

"Everyone, huh?" He stepped closer. "Everyone who?"

I shrugged. "People. TV. Sons of Anarchy."

He dropped his head back and laughed. "Fuck me, you're adorable."

"Am I wrong?"

"No," he admitted. "But *I'm* a one-woman man, so my whoring ways stop when I'm committed."

"To an asylum?"

He grinned. "Yeah, baby. Don't get to whore around in an asylum either."

I studied him for a few seconds, then blurted out, "My friend is dying."

He leaned back and frowned. "No shit?"

The tears overtook me again and I pushed away.

"Rem, come here," he demanded.

"I can't," I whispered.

"How come?"

"Because I need some distance and if I go there, I won't want you to stop holding me."

"Kind of what I'm counting on," he admitted with a smile.

I walked back to him, dropping my head to his chest and wrapping my arms around his waist. "Stay," I whispered, kissing his throat.

His mouth landed on mine and he lifted me high enough to wrap my legs around his waist as he slid one hand under my shirt and the other under my ass. I cupped his face and panted out, "Bedroom."

"Which way?"

"End of hall."

I kissed him again as he carried me to my room, dropping me gently on the bed and removing his cut and T-shirt. I let out a quiet gasp. God, this man was perfect. His left pec and bicep were covered with a detailed Celtic-tribal tattoo and a Dogs of Fire tattoo covered his right pec.

"You have a new tattoo," I observed. "Is that your club?"

"Yeah." He pushed my T-shirt up and kissed my belly.

I shivered as his tongue dipped into my belly button. "I love it."

"Yeah?" he whispered as his mouth moved up my

body.

"Yes."

He slid my shirt up further and he ran his tongue over my nipple. "You wanna keep talkin' about tattoos, Rem? Or do you want me to fuck you?"

I squirmed, trying to get closer. "You can't do both?"

His eyes met mine and he grinned. "Forgot how funny you were in bed."

"I'm funny all the time."

He neither confirmed nor denied as he straightened, wrapping his hands around the waistband of my sweats and tugging them down my legs, panties and all. He threw the discarded clothing into the corner of the room and pushed my knees up, spreading my legs and kissing his way down my inner thigh.

His mouth landed on my mound and I ripped off my shirt and wove my fingers into his hair as he sucked gently, before running his tongue between my folds. I moaned as he moved to my clit and sucked.

"You like that, huh?"

I nodded as I licked my lips and arched against his mouth, and he rewarded me with another suck. He slid a finger inside of me as he continued to suck, running the digit along my walls.

"Merrick, I'm…"

"Come, baby."

I didn't want to yet. I really didn't, but he played my body like Monopoly and I couldn't stop myself from passing go and collecting my two-hundred-dollar orgasm.

He removed his fingers and licked them before removing his jeans and boots, his dick springing free and my womb contracted with need. I bit my lip as he rolled a condom on and hovered above me. "You still like it hard?"

Goosebumps broke out over my skin and I nodded.

"You want it hard now?"

"Yes," I rasped, grabbing his arms. "Immediately."

He slid into me…slowly.

"Tweety," I growled, wrapping my legs around his waist and arching up against him.

He grinned, pressing in deeper. "Still impatient, I see."

Anchoring himself with one hand on the bed, he slid the other between our bodies and fingered my clit. I whimpered again, my need quickly becoming an obsession, and then he moved. Slow and deep, pressing his finger harder each time he buried himself.

"Merrick!" I cried out as an orgasm began a slow roll.

He didn't let me enjoy it. No. This time I was forced to pass go without collecting my two-hundred-dollar orgasm and straight to jail as he removed the hand between us, linking it with mine and dragging it over my head.

"Merr," I whimpered.

His mouth covered mine, cutting off any further complaint and he slammed into me. I hooked my legs around him tighter and he rewarded my action with his dick buried deeper and harder as he continued to kiss me.

Holding my hands hostage above my head, he thrust further and further into me, his tongue sliding against mine as his dick drove my pussy to new heights of pleasure. I screamed against his mouth as I came, tugging on his grip so I could touch him, and when he released me, I clawed at his back as my climax continued to swamp me.

He wasn't far behind me and I felt his cock pulse, then he kissed me again before rolling us onto our sides, facing each other and staying connected. Stroking my cheek, he smiled. "I fucking missed you, baby."

I nodded, unable to find my voice.

"You okay?"

I nodded again.

"Glad you're back, Rem."

The sting of tears hit my nose, but I bit back the sadness and forced a smile. "Me too."

"Gonna get rid of the rubber, then we're gonna do this again, yeah?"

"Yes, please," I rasped. I needed more. STAT.

Finch

THE NEXT AFTERNOON, after a relatively mild ball-busting by my Prez, I left the compound and headed to Remi's. I was surprised Crow hadn't sanctioned me or worse. I know I'd crossed the line breaking Vitaly's kneecap, but I couldn't honestly say I wouldn't do it again. And if Hatch hadn't stopped me, I can't honestly say I wouldn't have broken the other one. In the end, the Prez had issued me some grunt work the recruits usually did and left it at that. Flea's sister, Katie, had looked at my hand and deemed it was probably bruised, not broken, but suggested I get an x-ray to be sure. I decided I'd ice for a couple of days and go from there.

Now all I wanted was to bury my dick inside my woman again.

The fact I was still on a high from my morning with

Remi was probably why I'd taken my punishment without complaint. I'd never met anyone like her and I couldn't wait to see her again…not just because of her fucking amazing body. I liked her. She was funny and smart, and didn't take shit from me.

I pulled up to her apartment building and removed my helmet as I walked up the stairs to her unit. Some creepy looking asshole was using a key to unlock her door.

"Hey!" I bellowed. "What the fuck are you doing?"

"Gotta clean out this unit," he said.

"That's my woman's unit, fuckhead. How about you check your notes?"

He pulled his phone out with a groan and checked the screen. "Your woman Remington Charles?"

"Yeah."

"She split, man."

"What do you mean?"

"She paid off her lease and told the manager to sell or donate whatever was left inside."

I scowled. What the fuck?

"Did she leave a forwarding address?"

"No," the guy said.

I gave him a chin lift and pulled my phone out, dialing Remi's number. It went straight to voicemail. "Rem, need you to call me back," I said, trying to keep my voice calm. "Some asshole's cleaning out your apartment."

I hung up and ten seconds later, my phone buzzed with a text from her.

Remi: It's okay, Merrick. I left. I'm sorry.

I turned on my heel and headed back to my bike, calling her again. When her voicemail answered, I swore. "Remington, what the fuck is going on? You need to call me. Just let me know where you are."

This time there was no return text, so I called my sister.

"Hey, big brother."

"Where's Remi?" I demanded.

"What do you mean?"

"She's gone."

"Gone where?"

I took a deep breath. "That's what I'm hoping you know."

"Wait, back up. I have no idea what you're talking about."

I filled her in on what I knew, and she let out a series of swear words I'd never heard from her before. "So, you didn't know?"

"No, I didn't fucking know," she snapped. "God, I'm so pissed right now."

"Picking up on that, sissy."

"You need to have Booker trace her ass and find out what the hell her problem is."

"Yeah, Gracie, I'm on it."

"Then you need to tie her to the bed or something."

I couldn't stop a laugh. "Sissy, I'm not tying her to the bed. Well, unless she asks me to."

"Then I will. Until she explains why the fuck she keeps running away."

I had a pretty good idea why she kept running away, but it was Remi's story to tell, so I stayed quiet. "I'm gonna let you go."

"Keep me posted."

"I will," I lied.

We rang off and I called Booker who started his trace. I headed back to my condo and threw my keys on the counter before pulling my phone out and checking the screen.

Nothing.

Fuck!

I tried her again, but got her voicemail, so I hung up and tried to figure out where she'd go. Only one place came to mind and that was 'home.' If her trust fund had been frozen, it was the logical conclusion.

And we had someone in common.

Sort of.

I pulled up my contacts and hit 'call.'

"Finch, brother," Alamo answered jovially. "How the fuck are ya?"

I'd gotten to know our Savannah Chapter Sergeant at Arms pretty well when I was working down there to help resolve a legal issue the Club had gotten pulled into. The trip had ended with my dick between Remi's legs, and it was unforgettable.

"I'm in a bind," I said.

"No shit?"

I filled him in on everything I knew about Remington's situation, keeping several things private for obvious reasons.

"Shit," Alamo breathed out. "Jazz knows Remi, I think. I'll talk to her."

"If she sees Remi, ask her not to say anything about me, yeah?"

"No problem, brother. Is Booker lookin' into her?"

"Yeah. Gotta get *my* eyes on her, though."

"I hear ya. Always room here if you need to do it in person."

I smiled. "Got a feeling that's gonna happen sooner than later."

"Figured," he said. "I'll talk to Jasmine and get back to you."

"Appreciate it."

"You need us to watch her?"

"Yeah, man, that'd be good."

"You got it."

Alamo hung up and I relaxed knowing my brothers would make sure she was safe until I could take over.

Remington

Nine days. That was how long I'd been home, and how long it had been since I'd heard from Merrick. He'd called a couple more times, but didn't leave another voicemail and I was both relieved and saddened by that fact. I missed him. Horribly. But I wasn't willing to drag him into my shit storm of a life. No one deserved that.

"Earth to Remi," Kennedy droned, snapping her fingers in front of me.

"Oh, sorry, what did I miss?" I asked, taking a sip of my margarita.

Michelle and Kennedy had organized girls' night out, and I'd insisted we avoid anywhere that one of Merrick's 'brothers' might frequent, but I couldn't stop scanning the space a hundred times a minute.

"You're missing everything," Kennedy said. "Like the guy staring at you…three o'clock."

I rolled my eyes. I didn't miss him at all. He just wasn't my type. "Pass," I said.

"She needs more booze," Michelle said, and I laughed.

"No amount of alcohol will make me want that guy." I slid out of the booth. "But I do need to pee. I'll be right back."

Grabbing my purse, I headed into the ladies' room and did my thing, then pulled open the door to head back to the table.

"Miss me, baby?"

I squeaked and tried to step back into the bathroom, but Merrick wrapped an arm around me like a vice and tugged me gently out. "Not this time."

Oh my god, he was here. Really here. I wanted to crawl inside his leather jacket and snuggle, but I refused to let him see my elation.

"What are you doing here?" I asked as he pushed me

against the wall.

"You seriously asking me that?" he challenged.

"Merrick," I whispered.

"Yeah, Rem?"

"What are you doing here?" I repeated.

"What did I tell you?"

I met his eyes. "When?"

"Right before I buried my dick in your pussy."

I dropped my head. "I don't remember," I lied.

"Cute, Rem."

"You shouldn't be here."

"You want me to leave?" He lifted my chin and frowned. "And be honest. Don't give me some bullshit answer that's gonna piss me off."

I licked my lips. "You don't have to stay."

He sighed, kissing me gently. "Pain in my ass."

I wrinkled my nose. "Hey, that's my line."

He shook his head. "You need to promise me you're gonna fucking stay put, Remi."

I gripped his jacket. "I promise, I won't run away from you again."

"You in this with me?"

I knew this question was one of finality, which meant I needed to make sure my answer was just as final. The truth was, this man had gotten under my skin…in a good way. But I was afraid to trust. Afraid I'd make yet another bad choice, and he'd hurt me.

"Rem?" He stroked my cheek, drawing my focus back to him.

I decided to take a leap of faith and breathed out, "Yes, Toucan Sam, I'm in this with you."

He raised an eyebrow. "Toucan Sam?"

"Because you're nosy."

He dropped his head back and laughed. "Fuck me."

"Yes, please."

He kissed me again. "We need to talk, so you're gonna

say goodnight to your friends and I'm gonna take you back to the compound."

"Compound?"

"Club."

"Is it a super-secret biker lair?"

"Don't think it's all that secret, but, sure, we can call it a lair."

I slid my hands up his chest. "Are you really here?"

"Yeah, baby, I'm really here."

"I'm so sorry, Merrick."

"We'll talk when we get somewhere quiet. You can explain everything to me then."

I frowned up at him. "Do you hate me?"

He stroked my cheek. "Do you think I'd be here if I hated you?"

I shrugged. "Promise me, that tonight, after I tell you everything, if you want out, you'll leave. Okay?"

"No."

"Tweety," I breathed out.

"Come on. Let's tell your friends you're leaving."

"Wait," I said, and gripped his jacket again. "One more."

He grinned as he leaned down to kiss me, then took my hand and walked me back to my table.

* * *

I was highly disappointed Merrick drove me to the lair in a very sensible rental car instead of a bike, but he'd said he got in a few hours ago and hadn't sorted out one to borrow.

"You really just got here?" I asked.

"Yeah. Flew in at seven."

"Why?"

He frowned at me as he stopped at a red light. "You seriously asking me that right now?"

God, I sound so fucking needy.

"Never mind."

He shook his head, facing forward again and we drove on. We didn't speak again until we arrived at a huge barn surrounded by tall fencing. He slid his window down and the guard gave him a chin lift and opened the gate for him.

Merrick had said that the compound was housed in an old tobacco barn on almost thirty acres, but there were newer, smaller buildings surrounding it. Fencing and concrete walls made the compound impenetrable, along with the armed men guarding it.

"I feel like we're heading into a jail."

"It's definitely as secure as one," Merrick said. "But you're free to go anytime you want to. In theory, anyway."

I smiled. "Brat."

He parked next to a couple of pickups and we headed inside. Linking his fingers with mine, he led me into a huge room and I let out a quiet whistle as I spun to take in everything.

The main room of the barn was all wood and open, probably like it had been back in the day. There were three sets of stairs, one off the main room, one off the kitchen at the back and one off the foyer.

"It's beautiful."

"Yeah, it's a hell of a lot cooler than Portland." He squeezed my hand. "But don't repeat that."

I grinned. "Lips are sealed."

"Finch, man. Hey."

We turned toward the voice and I saw a tall, dark and bearded man walking toward us, holding a beer. God, he was gorgeous.

"Hey, Alamo. Jasmine kick you out?" Merrick joked.

Oh! Alamo. This is the man who killed Thomas.

Alamo chuckled. "She's on her way here, actually. This must be Remington."

"Hi," I rasped, finding it hard to find my voice.

"You okay?" Alamo asked.

I bobbed my head up and down. "Yep."

"Sorry I'm late," a feminine voice called out as she rushed for Alamo and wrapped her arms around his neck.

"Hey, Firefly." He grinned, leaning down to kiss her. I recognized Jasmine immediately. Her red hair gave her away.

Jasmine Buckley was gorgeous. Curvy, sassy, her red hair matching her personality perfectly, and she was sweet. Not a pushover, but very kind.

She turned to face us and pulled Merrick in for a hug. "Hey, Finch."

"Hey, Jazz. Have you met Remington?"

"Once," she said with a smile.

"The Children's Hospital benefit, right?"

She nodded. "Exactly. Such a weird night."

I chuckled. "Right?"

Merrick raised an eyebrow in question and I squeezed his hand. I'd fill him in later.

"But I also saw you dance at school one year," Jasmine said. "You were amazing."

"Oh, thanks."

"Gonna show Remi around," Merrick said, and Alamo gave him a chin lift as Merrick led me out of the main room and upstairs.

"Explain how a charity dinner can be weird," Merrick said, as he pushed open a door and stepped back.

I walked inside and smiled. "The chairman's wife, who was sixty-two at the time, got wasted drunk and gave a speech accusing several of the women in the room of 'fucking' her man. Jasmine's dad had to virtually carry her off the stage."

"Holy shit."

"Exactly. They stayed together, though. Because, you know, it would look bad if they divorced."

Merrick chuckled. "Rich people are fuckin' weird."

I nodded. "Definitely."

"I was referring to you."

"Like hell you were. I'm not rich."

Merrick laughed. "Yeah, you are. I didn't realize how rich until I got your money back, but you're definitely rich."

"Wait, what?"

"We got your money back."

"How?"

"Can't tell you that."

"Why not? It's my money."

"Club business." He pulled out his wallet and handed me a card. "This has all your new banking information. We moved it so your parents couldn't find it."

"Oh my god, are you serious?" I whispered.

"Yeah."

"Why?"

"Not gonna dignify that with a response," he said, and opened the mini fridge by the window, pulling out a beer.

"Merrick, please. Why would you do that? I've been a total bitch to you."

"Again. Not gonna digni—"

I let out a frustrated groan.

He held his arm out. "Come here."

"Did you do this because you felt some weird obliga-tion—"

He waved his hand. "Come here, Rem."

"I—"

"Swear to Christ, woman, you don't get your ass over here so I can hold you, I'm gonna turn you over my knee."

I swallowed.

"Remi," he growled.

"I'm not sure which one I want more," I admitted and found my mouth covered with his.

I touched my tongue to his and wrapped my arms around his waist before breaking the kiss and meeting his eyes. "I'm really sorry, Merr."

"Accepted. You wanna talk now or fuck?"

"Fuck," I breathed out. "Definitely fuck."

He grinned. "I was hoping you'd say that."

Setting the beer on the windowsill, he lifted me and dropped me gently onto the bed, crawling up my body to kiss me before unzipping my jeans. "So fucking beautiful, Remington."

"Back atya, Tweety."

"You in this?"

I nodded.

"Need to hear the words, Rem. Figured out a little later than I should that if I don't hear the words, you're not making a deal."

I bit back a smile. "I'm in this, Merrick Lundy, AKA Tweety, AKA Big Bird, AKA Toucan Sam. I won't run again. I promise…Hei Hei."

"You done?"

"Yep…Chicken Little…AKA Scrooge McDuck."

He dropped his head to my chest and his shoulders shook as he laughed. "Fuck, Rem."

"Yes, please, Foghorn…show me your Leghorn."

"You keep making me laugh, I'm not gonna be able to fuck you."

I slid my hand between us, cupping his already rock-hard cock. "Well, that's a lie…Zazu."

"How many fucking cartoons did you watch as a kid?"

"Who said I watched cartoons as a kid?" I challenged, slipping the button on his jeans and sliding the zipper down.

"You a secret cartoon watcher?" he asked, lifting his hips slightly so I'd have better access to his body.

"I don't know how secret it is."

He let out a quiet hiss when I moved the waistband of his boxers aside and wrapped my hand around his cock, running my tongue over his bottom lip.

"On your back, honey," I ordered. "I need to taste you."

He rolled onto his back, removing the rest of his clothing before settling into place. I grinned, tugging off my shirt and unhooking my bra, freeing my breasts but keeping my jeans on. "Do not touch," I ordered.

He linked his fingers together, sliding his hands up and resting his head in them with a grin. I stepped off the bed to remove the rest of my clothes, then knelt between his legs. He reached for me, but I smacked his hands. "No touching," I growled.

"You gonna let my dick fuck your tits?" he asked.

I raised an eyebrow. "If you let me finish."

He settled his hands behind his head again. "Continue."

I ran my tongue up his shaft, then guided the tip into my mouth. Merrick pulled his knees up and I wrapped an arm around one of his thighs as I worked his cock with my mouth and free hand. His hands slid into my hair and I frowned at him but continued to suck. He released my hair and placed his hands behind his head again. I took him deeper into my mouth and he closed his eyes and shifted up slightly.

I gripped the base of his shaft with one hand, and pumped with the motion of my mouth, cupping his balls gently.

"Fuck, Rem," he rasped.

His legs straightened, and his sac tightened, and I knew he was close.

"Now, baby," he rasped, drawing his knees up again and I took him deeper as he came, swallowing then releasing him with a loud 'smack.'

He chuckled as he smiled down at me. I crawled up his body, kissing him as I went, then settled beside him, snuggling close. "I didn't think you were going to let me finish."

"Well, if I'd known you were gonna lie to me, I wouldn't have."

"How did I lie?"

"You said my dick was gonna fuck your tits."

"Oh, it will, Tweety," I promised, kissing his chest. "We have all night."

"Are you trying to distract me?"

"From what?"

"Talking."

I shook my head. "No. We can talk, I just want something to remember you by."

He lifted my chin. "Stop it."

"Merr, I'm being serious. I won't be mad."

He sat up. "Goddammit, Remington, I'm not going anywhere. Just drop it."

I sighed, dragging my hands down my face as he stalked into the bathroom. I heard the toilet flush, then the faucet start, then he was walking back to the bed. God, he was gorgeous.

"You got some drool right there," he said, tapping his finger on the corner of my mouth.

I wrinkled my nose. "I can't help it. You're delicious."

He grinned, kneeling on the bed and kissing me. "Back atya."

Merrick stretched out again and pulled me over his chest. "Fill me in, Rem. All of it."

SEVEN

Remington

I TOLD MERRICK about my conversation with Michelle and her never ending battle with cancer, ending up in a blubbering mess as I said out loud that my friend was going to die…and it was going to be soon.

As my shitty experiences of late washed over me, I sobbed into his chest and let him hold me as I poured out my heart. I felt like I'd tried to do everything right and I'd been a colossal failure. I'd picked the man my parents approved of, I'd followed my dreams and uprooted my life to move to a city I'd never been to in order to bring those dreams to fruition, and I'd tried to be a good friend and daughter. Everything was a mess and I didn't know how to right the wrong.

"I mean, why the fuck do men think it's okay to beat the shit out of me?" I asked, rhetorically. "Or control me somehow? My father, my boyfriends, my brother when he decides he's going to be a dick. Okay, maybe not Dawson…he's not really a dick. He just tries to 'protect' me and ends up inserting himself where he doesn't belong. But still, he's barely two years older than me, so he has no right to talk."

Merrick gave me a gentle squeeze.

"Are you saying nothing because you like to insert yourself where you don't belong?" I challenged, then clarified, "With Grace, I mean."

"Nice save," he said with a chuckle.

"Well, you do it to me as well, but I like it. Mostly."

Merrick rolled me so I was on my back and he was hovering over me, running his thumb over my cheek. "You done crying?"

I shrugged.

He smiled gently. "Just want to make sure you hear me."

I sniffed loudly, then nodded.

"You got a chance to do that swab test thingy for your friend, right?"

"Well, sort of. I take the swab and then they let me know if I can donate marrow or stem cells or whatever, then I have to go in and do the blood thing. I might be a match for someone, but I can't just give it to Michelle, even if she and I are a match."

"Yeah, baby, I get it. But you could help someone else."

"Yes. Definitely. But, if I'm being honest, I'm selfish and I just want to help her."

"I'm sure that's how most people feel."

"I'm willing to do anything, though, if it gives her a few more years, you know?" I rasped.

"Yeah, I know."

"I signed up. I'm just waiting for the swab."

"You want me to sign up too?"

"You would do that?" I asked, my heart filling.

"Sure. Why not?"

"Oh my god, you are the best human on the planet," I whispered, then burst into tears again.

He chuckled, pulling me close again and dragging the covers over us. "Okay, baby. I got you."

"I'm falling in love with you," I whispered into his throat. "It's why I didn't tell you I was leaving. I'm sorry."

"For falling in love with me or leaving?"

"Both."

"I forgive you," he said with a cheeky grin, then kissed me gently. "I'm sorry your friend is sick."

"Me too."

"We'll both donate if we can, okay?"

I nodded. "That'd be good, Merr."

"You hungry?"

"I am if pizza's on the table."

He grinned. "Pizza's always on the table."

"Then I want combo."

"Okay, I'll order combo."

"With anchovies."

"No."

"Why not?" I challenged.

He shook his head and slid out of bed. "Not gonna dignify that with a response."

"You don't want my fishy mouth all over your body?" I leaned up on my arms. "Come on, Scuttle, live a little."

He dragged on his jeans and pulled his phone out of the pocket. "Who the fuck is Scuttle?"

"Disney seagull, from the Little Mermaid." He rolled his eyes and I grinned. "I nannied for a family during the summers for a few years in college. I'm well-versed in all things Disney, among others."

"Apparently." He texted something into his phone, then leaned over me and kissed me gently. "I'll be right back."

"Where are you going?"

"Gonna grab some drinks, only got beer in the fridge, and grab the pizza when it gets here."

"I can help."

"Nah, it's good. You hang here and relax."

"Do you have wine?"

"I'll look," he said, snagging his shirt off the floor and heading for the door.

"And plates and napkins."

"Got it." He smiled at me over his shoulder. "Text me if you think of anything else."

"Oh, I will, Tweety." I slid my legs off the bed. "Chocolate."

He laughed. "Text me, baby."

"Fine," I said with a huff. "Hurry."

"I can't do that if you don't let me leave."

I flicked my hands toward him. "Shoo."

He laughed again and walked out the door.

* * *

Finch

I pulled my T-shirt over my head as I walked downstairs. Goddammit, my woman was funny as shit. When she wasn't being crazy. But I loved her crazy.

Fuck.

I stopped walking.

I love her.

I shook my head and headed into the kitchen where I found Alamo and Jasmine making out. I cleared my throat and Jazz tried to jump away, but Alamo held tight with a chuckle. "Not doin' anything wrong, Firefly."

She shook her head. "I know. I just forget sometimes. Hi, Finch."

"Hey." I grinned and stepped to the fridge. "Do we have any wine anywhere?"

"In the pantry," Jasmine said. "Willow and I bring a

couple of bottles every get together. Only red, though."

I smiled. "That's all Remi'll drink."

"Perfect, then."

"I'll replace it this week," I promised.

"No rush."

I stepped into the huge pantry and found a bottle that would work, then noticed bars of chocolate next to graham crackers and marshmallows, so I snagged her some chocolate. I walked back into the kitchen and set everything on the huge stainless-steel island.

"Is Remington okay?" Jasmine asked.

"She will be," I said.

Jasmine smiled. "Wine will help."

I chuckled. "Yeah, that's what I'm hoping. I also ordered pizza, so gonna put her into a wine and carb coma."

"Good plan," Alamo said, and Jasmine smacked his arm. He grinned and pulled her close again. "It's how I calm the feral Firefly when needed."

She jabbed a finger toward me. "Do not listen to any advice from him on how to treat your girlfriend, Finch." She turned her frown on Alamo. "And, you and me? Well, we're going to have a conversation later when we're alone."

"You gonna be naked when we do that?"

"No."

"Well, shit," Alamo hissed. "That doesn't bode well for me."

"No, no it doesn't," Jasmine said, but she winked at me and I knew she was messing with him.

"Alamo, over." A voice crackled over the walkie, and Alamo grabbed it off the counter.

"Go ahead."

"Pizza order."

"Go ahead and pay for it," he said. "Finch'll come get it."

"Got it."

I gave Alamo a chin lift, then headed out to the front gate where I retrieved the pizza and paid Stump back. As I walked back into the compound, my phone buzzed in my pocket and I pulled it out to find a text from Remi.

Pickles.

I bit back a grin as I texted back: Is that another bird, or do you want pickles?

I want pickles. And ice cream.

Are you pregnant?

Oh, ha ha.

This was followed by an emoji flipping me off.

I laughed, then went searching for some pickles…which were, surprisingly, in the pantry. There were several choices of ice cream in the freezer, so I grabbed mint chocolate chip. I had a feeling I was going to be replacing a shit ton of food by the time Remi left.

I found a grocery bag and filled it with what I'd collected, then headed back upstairs, pushing open the door to find the bed empty. "Rem?"

"Bathroom," she called, then walked out and I frowned. "What's wrong?"

"I left you in my bed, naked, and now you're not."

She grinned. "Panties don't count."

Fuck, they did so count, and, it was all she wore. Her perfect tits were on display but the tiny wisp of lace hiding her pussy was what drove me a little crazy. Goddamn I was already hard.

I closed the distance between us and wrapped an arm around her waist. "They're not staying on."

"Good. Food first, though." She kissed me. "Did you find pickles?"

"Yeah, I found the pickles. You have weird cravings."

"Can you imagine what I'll be like when I'm actually pregnant?"

"You want kids?"

"Yes. Don't you?"

I shrugged. "Haven't really thought about it."

She leaned back. "Really?"

"Has Grace told you about our mom?"

"No. I mean, I know she's no longer alive, but that's all."

I opened the pizza box and waved to a chair. "Eat, baby. We'll talk after."

EIGHT

Remington

W E ATE. IN silence. Which made me nervous, and I hated it. I set my elbow on the little table and rested my head in my palm. "Are you okay?" I asked.

"Yeah. Are you?"

I shook my head. "What happened with your mom?"

He sighed, leaning back in his chair and taking a swig of beer. "Long story short, she took Grace hostage and then shot herself in the head."

"In front of Grace?" I rasped.

"Yep."

I bit back tears. "Why?"

"Mom was schizophrenic, among other things. She stopped taking her meds and all hell broke loose. The problem was, she'd convinced my dad she was back on her schedule, but he thinks now she was taking them, then making herself puke. He always watched her take them, then checked her mouth, so he knew she wasn't cheeking them."

He seemed to fade into the story, so I stayed as quiet as I could in order not to interrupt his flow.

"Dad had promised to take me to a movie and Grace had begged to come, but Mom wanted a girl day, and honestly, I wanted time with my dad, without my annoying little sister." He shook his head. "I shoulda fuckin' objected."

I scooted my chair closer to him and slid my hands up his thighs.

"Mom locked her and Grace in the bathroom and held a gun to her fucking head. If Mom hadn't called her best friend, Maisie, Mom would have killed my sister. Instead she blew her fucking brains out in front of Grace. She was covered in grey matter and bone fragments, and stuck in the bathroom with our mother's body until EMS got there. Then she was prodded and poked by the doctors and nurses, and would only let Maisie anywhere near her."

I felt tears streaming down my face as I climbed onto his lap and wrapped my arms around his neck. "I'm so sorry, honey."

"I'm okay. It's Grace that's the fucking rock star. My sister's the strongest person I know. She's had to deal with a lot of shit, PTSD, night terrors, the whole deal, but she still graduated with a four-point-o and opened herself up to Flea."

"That's good," I said.

He gave me a sad smile and nodded. "Yeah. It's good."

"Were you close to your mom?"

"Yeah. Can't talk about that around Grace, though," he said.

I stroked his cheek. "That's gotta be hard, honey. Not to talk about her with your sister."

"Sometimes." He sighed. "But the good memories are tainted for her, so I get that."

"God, you're a good man, Merrick."

"You think so?"

"I know so," I whispered, and kissed him.

He cupped my breast and rolled the nipple into a tight bud, his tongue dipping into my mouth as I shifted to straddle him. His hand slid between my legs, shifting the lace of my panties aside and pressing his fingers into me. I ground down against him as he held me anchored to his body.

Breaking our kiss, he sucked a nipple into his mouth, then blew on the wetness before doing the same to the other one. I arched against his mouth as he fucked me with his fingers, his thumb connecting with my clit as I continued to grind on him.

His fingers swept against my walls, one whispering over my G-spot and I dropped my head back with a moan. "*Don't* move," I ordered, shifting to take him deeper.

I felt my climax building, but when he bit down gently on my nipple, I exploded around him, gripping the back of the chair for balance. "Oh my god," I rasped, and he slid his hand out from between my legs.

"Love how your body responds, baby," he said, and kissed me.

"Love how you work my body into a frenzy."

He grinned, standing as he kept me in his arms and dropping me gently onto the bed. "Gonna do that again."

"That'd be appreciated, honey."

After stripping off his clothes, he slid my panties down my legs and threw them in the corner, kneeling between my legs and kissing the inside of my thighs. "On your knees, Remi."

I rolled over and repositioned myself onto all-fours, hearing the quiet tear of foil before Merrick's dick teased the opening of my pussy. I pushed back to try and get relief, but Merrick's hand on my ass gave me an indication that was not going to happen.

"Tweety," I rasped.

His hand slipped between my legs and I ground down against it. "You need to be patient."

"Fuck patience," I growled. He slapped his palm against my pussy and I cried out with need. "Honey, please."

"You like that?"

Another slap.

"God, yes," I whispered.

"You want more?"

"No, I want your cock."

He removed his hand and pushed into me and I almost came right then and there, but then he moved, and I was once again swept away.

"Merr," I panted out as he slammed into me harder and harder with each pass.

"Now, baby," he ordered, and I came.

Hard.

We fell together onto the mattress and he pulled me close, kissing the back of my neck. "You still like it rough, I see."

I grinned. "Guilty."

"It's one of my favorite things about you."

"Oh, really?"

"Among others." He kissed my neck again and slid out of me, heading to the bathroom, but returning quickly to pull me back into his arms.

"What others?" I asked, rolling to face him.

He grinned, stroking my cheek as he studied me. "Your fierceness, for one."

"You think I'm fierce?"

"The fiercest," he said, and kissed me. "Love your sass, but you know that already."

"You can say it again, it's okay."

He chuckled. "I love your body, but I think I've proven that quite a few times lately."

"I kinda love your body, too."

"I'm picking up on that."

"I love you, Rem."

"You do?"

"Yeah. Knew it the second you jumped into your super fancy karate stance."

I bit my lip and closed my eyes. "Say it again," I whispered.

"I love your super fancy karate stance."

I smacked his chest gently and frowned at him. "In case you haven't noticed, I'm feeling insecure and needy, and since I've never done a day of any kind of martial arts, there's no way I have a 'super fancy karate stance.'"

He kissed my nose. "Wish I'd had my camera out. Woulda loved to have videoed it."

I rolled my eyes and tried to shift away from him, but his arm snaked around my waist. "Where are you going?"

"Back to the Dojo so I can learn how to wax on…or sweep the leg…or whatever."

He let out a bellow of a laugh and held me tighter. "Fuck me, baby, you're so fucking funny."

"Yeah? Happy you think so," I retorted. "Can I go pee now?"

"In a second."

"Tweety," I warned.

"Look at me, Rem."

I met his eyes with a huff.

"I love you. You're funny, you're beautiful, you're kind, and you're fucking sexy as hell. I'm pretty sure I fell in love with you the second I saw you laughing with your friends, but it was solidified when you gave me all of you our first night together."

"I didn't give you all of me," I lied.

"Bullshit."

"I'm just a friendly person."

"Not that friendly."

"You don't know me."

"I know you," he argued.

I snuggled closer. "I *want* you to know me."

"I already know you."

"Merrick."

"Yeah, baby?"

"You're being ornery."

He rolled me onto my back and kissed me. "You love it."

"Do I?"

"Trust me, baby. I know you."

I rolled my eyes. "Oh my god."

"My name's Finch, baby. Not God."

"Jebus."

He kissed me again. "Nope, still Finch."

"Tweety."

"Or Tweety. But only to you."

I bit back a laugh. "You are ridiculous."

"You think?" he asked, kissing his way down my body.

When he reached my pussy, he ran his tongue over my clit. "Still think I'm ridiculous?"

I stared at him and raised an eyebrow. "That depends on whether or not you're gonna dial it up a notch or stop." His tongue flicked out and I groaned. "Tweety."

"Yeah, baby? Do you need something?"

I squirmed and tried to shove down my need. "Nope. I'm good."

He slid a finger inside of me. "You sure?"

I swallowed convulsively, but managed to nod. "Yep."

Adding another finger, he sucked my clit again, running his tongue along my folds.

"Merr—"

"Yeah, baby?"

I licked my lips. "Nothing. Never mind."

He shifted so he was kneeling between my legs and rolled on a condom. "You gonna tell me what you want?"

"You know me so well, you tell me."

He chuckled, hovering above me and pressing the tip of his cock against my entrance. "Challenge accepted," he retorted and pushed into me.

I bit my lip and forced myself not to react. God, I loved every second of what he was currently doing to me.

"Nothing, huh?" he taunted.

"No, it feels good, honey. Keep going. You'll get it," I condescended in my best teacher voice.

"Jesus Christ, woman, you make me laugh right now, we're gonna have a problem."

"Oh, no," I deadpanned. "You can't keep it up and laugh at the same time? Do I need to hide some Viagra in an edible to help give you the giggles *and* a boner?"

"I've got a big ol' blunt for you…," he thrust into me, "…right here."

I gasped as his girth filled me. "We could market it as the 'Bone-a-laugh.'"

"Or 'Funnyboner.'" He pushed in further.

I mewed as I gripped his arms and forced myself not to chuckle.

"You gonna let me fuck you now?" he challenged, raising an eyebrow.

"Are you gonna do it hard?"

"You wanna be on your knees, Remi?"

I nodded, and he slid out of me, so I could readjust. Once I was on my knees, he pushed into me again and I spread to take him deeper. He gripped my hips and slammed into me faster and faster and I whimpered as my orgasm built. He slapped my ass once…then twice and I exploded around him as he continued to bury himself deep.

"Fuck, Rem," he growled as he thrust in again, building another orgasm in me and I pushed back against him to take him deeper.

"Yes, baby," I rasped as he slid his hand between my legs and fingered my clit.

"Come, Remi."

I came, and he pulled his cock out and settled against my ass, the warmth of his cum covering me as he guided us back onto the mattress.

"Oh my god," I whispered.

He kissed my shoulder. "Yeah."

I rolled to face him. "I don't want you to leave."

"Baby, I just got here," he said, and slid out of bed, heading to the bathroom. "I'm not leaving right away."

I followed.

Merrick started the shower then faced me. "You joining me?"

"Yes," I said. "But we need to talk about this."

"I'm here for two weeks, Rem. Unless the club needs me back, I'm good. I don't have any pressing cases, and whatever work I need to do now, I can do here."

"Then what?"

"Guess than depends on you."

"What if I'd told you to fuck off?"

"Then I would have left," he said, and stepped into the shower, holding his hand out to me.

I took it and stepped in beside him. "Are you going to stay longer than two weeks?"

"No."

"Why not?"

"Because I can't, honey," he said, dropping his head back, under the water.

I sighed. "No, I get it."

"But you're coming back with me, so I don't know what you're freaking out about."

"I can't go back with you."

"Why not?" he asked, guiding me under the water.

"Because I just got back." I settled my hands on his waist as he poured shampoo onto my head and began to massage it into my scalp.

"Exactly. Which means, you can come back with me

and it won't fuck up anything."

I closed my eyes. "Um, hello. I gave up my apartment."

"Um, hello…I own my own condo."

"I can't move in with you."

"You can't?"

I opened one eye, then closed it so soap wouldn't get in it. "Are you asking?"

"Yeah, sure, if you need me to ask," he said, guiding my hair back under the water.

"I can't."

"Why not?"

"Because we don't know each other."

He didn't say anything as he rinsed my hair, so I wiped my face and opened my eyes. "Tweety?"

"Not gonna—"

"Dignify that with a response?" I finished.

He grinned, kissing my nose. "She's getting it."

"Merrick, we've fucked a dozen times over the span of a couple of days, that does not mean we know each other."

He picked up the bottle of conditioner and squeezed some into his palm, then massaged it through my hair.

"Are you really not going to say anything?" I snapped.

"Remington, I have to head back to Portland in two weeks. I want you to come with me, but that's ultimately your choice. Not gonna force you if you don't want to." He tipped my head back. "Rinse."

I rinsed, then wiped my face again. "I don't know if I can just pick up and move again."

He shrugged.

The asshole just shrugged!

"Seriously?" I hissed.

"Don't," he warned.

"Don't what?"

"Spiral, Remington," he said. "I love you. So much so, I followed you here. If you can't make it work to move back with me in two weeks, we'll figure something out.

There's no pressure."

I dropped my head to his chest. "How are you so fuck-ing calm about all of this?"

He slid his hands to my neck and lifted my chin. "We've got two weeks to spend together, baby. It's plenty of time to figure shit out. I'm in. Are you?"

"Yes," I breathed out. "I'm just worried you're going to leave and I'm going to be stuck here without you."

"Okay, Eeyore. You go towel off and we'll watch a movie and eat dessert."

"I'm not Eeyore."

"You are most definitely Eeyore." He gave my butt a playful smack, then kissed me.

"I am *not* clinically depressed."

He chuckled. "No, but you are the nervous type…probably more akin to Piglet, but I'm figuring you'd be offended if I called you a pig."

"So, I'm an ass?"

He grinned. "Maybe we should take this conversation out of the Hundred-Acre Wood and find something to eat."

"Probably a good idea. Can't imagine you in Christo-pher Robin's shorts."

He kissed me gently and then I climbed out and tow-eled off.

"I wish I'd brought a change of clothes," I complained once he was out of the shower.

He raised an eyebrow. "See you found a pair of my un-derwear."

I grinned. I'd rummaged in one of his bags and found them, along with a T-shirt. "Yep. They're a little big, but they're comfy."

He slid his arm around my waist and cupped my ass. "They're yours now, baby. Don't say I never gave you any-thing."

I tugged on the towel around his waist and grinned as it fell to the floor. "I'm thinking I should show my gratitude."

I knelt before him and ran my tongue along his cock.

Before anything could get interesting, however, someone banged on his door.

"What?" he bellowed.

"All-hands, Finch. Meeting room."

"Fuck," he snapped, then called out, "Be down in a sec."

"Why do *you* need to go?" I asked. "This isn't your chapter."

He stroked my cheek and helped me to my feet. "I'm part of the brotherhood, baby, so when Prez calls an all-hands, I'm there."

I wrinkled my nose. "Oh."

"Let me figure out what's going on. Stay here, okay?"

I nodded, and he dressed quickly, then left me half-dressed and horny.

NINE

Finch

I WALKED INTO the main meeting room that looked so much like our own in Portland. The walls were adorned with flags and banners collected over decades. The spoils of rallies and runs of the past. Harley calendars dating back to before models had fake tits were pinned up here and there.

Alamo was standing by the window, a drink in his hand, and a scowl on his face, and that scowl was directed at the chapter president.

"We don't know that for sure," Doc said.

"Like hell we don't," Alamo growled. "Dalton said these aren't copycats, so what other conclusion can we come to?"

"What's going on?" I asked.

"We don't know just yet because we don't have all the

information," Doc said, aiming his words at Alamo even more than me. "Dalton Moore, our guy who still has an 'in' at the F.B.I., reached out to Alamo today. He wanted to give us a head's up that two bodies have been found that appear to be in connection with the Gentleman Strangler."

"Jesus, Thomas Ellis killed even more women?" I asked.

Doc and Alamo exchanged a look before Doc continued. "That's the thing. These are new murders.

"New? But how? Thomas is dead. Alamo shot him," I said.

"Thanks for the fuckin' news flash Walter Cronkite," Alamo said before taking a shot of bourbon.

"Don't be a dick to the kid," Doc said. "All we know is that two more bodies have been found, one in our area, and one in Beaver County, Oklahoma. Dalton wouldn't give us much more information, but the F.B.I. is convinced these killings are related, and that they are not the work of a copycat."

"So, what does that mean?" I asked.

"It fuckin' means I killed the wrong man," Alamo grunted while pouring another drink.

"Ease up, Alamo," Doc said.

"Pretty fucking sure you didn't kill the wrong man," I retorted.

"First of all," Doc continued. "Thomas was a piece of shit and was definitely involved in the murders, if not a direct participant. The F.B.I. has way too much evidence to say otherwise, not to mention everything we know about him personally."

"Then who the hell killed these women?" Badger asked.

"And what did we miss?" Alamo followed up.

"We didn't miss anything," Doc said.

"Then, how the fuck do we explain two more women being raped and murdered in the exact same fashion after I put a bullet into that sick fuck? There's obviously someone else out there who's working with Thomas. Hell, as far as we know, he's the one that's been in charge this whole time. Jasmine could be in danger all over again and we don't even have the slightest clue who we should be protecting her from!" Alamo shouted and launched his glass across the room, causing it to shatter into pieces against the back wall.

"For fuck's sake Alamo!" Doc bellowed and shielded his eyes from the flying shards. "We're all concerned here."

"I'm far from concerned, Doc," Alamo said. "I'm pissed off that piece of shit Thomas is fucking with Jasmine from the grave, and I'm pissed off that there's another one of these sick bastards out there."

"Then let's figure out what we're gonna do about it," Doc said.

* * *

Remington

Merrick texted to tell me he was gonna be a while, so I decided to clean his room. Pulling on a pair of sweats, I stepped into the hallway to see if I could find some sheets but ran into Jasmine instead.

"Hey," she said. "I was just coming to find you."

"You were?" I asked.

"A couple of us are watching a movie. Want to join?"

"I take it, this "all-hands" is going to take a while?"

"They usually do."

I smiled. "Then, I'd love to watch a movie. Let me grab my phone."

I walked back into Merrick's room and threw on a bra, grabbed my phone, and slid on a pair of his socks before following Jasmine downstairs and into a huge movie room.

"Oh my god, Remington Charles?"

I squinted my eyes in the dim light. "Quinlan West-gate?"

My old friend pulled me in for a hug. "What are you doing here?"

"She's with Finch," Jasmine provided.

"Grace's brother?"

"Yes," I said.

"Is he here?"

"Yes," I said again.

Quin smiled. "Well, that sounds like a story and a half…maybe we should wait to start the movie."

"What are *you* doing here?" I asked.

"Well, that's *also* a story and a half…"

The movie was paused, the wine was poured, and we filled each other in until our men came to find us two hours later.

* * *

Finch

"And he hit her, Merrick. Beat her to shit over and over again."

My woman was drunk. And emotional. And currently pacing my room raging at Quin's ex-husband who was a piece of shit.

"Yeah, honey, I know," I said, handing her a bottled water.

Our meeting had wrapped up an hour ago and we'd headed into the media room to find our women crying. All of them. Four bottles of wine annihilated, and five women all gathered around Quinlan, sobbing as they hugged her.

I'd peeled Remington away from the group, led her upstairs, and was currently trying to figure out how to get her to calm down and hydrate.

"Why didn't you stop it?" she snapped.

"Baby, I wasn't here. I just know that shit went down

90

with her and her ex. Alamo and Badger ran him out of town."

"He *raped* her, Merrick. More than once. And you said you'd leave."

"When?"

"When you got here. You said if I told you to leave, you would have," she cried. "Did you mean it?"

I smiled gently. "What do you think?"

"I think you would have broken down any door and busted through any wall that kept me from you."

"Yeah, baby. You're right."

"I know I'm right," she said with a sniff. "I'm always right. I'm the fucking queen."

"Rem?"

She licked her lips. "What?"

"Gonna hold you now, okay?"

She nodded, and I closed the distance between us, wrapping my arms around her. She dropped the water bottle on the bed and slid her hands under my shirt, squeezing me tight.

"He almost killed Badger," she whispered.

"I know, baby."

"To make her obey him."

"Yeah," I said with a sigh. "He's a piece of shit."

"And then he raped her to drive home his threat."

I stroked her hair and kissed her temple.

"How is she still functioning?" she asked.

"People might ask you the same thing," I said.

"Having your ex-fiancé demand to shit on your tits does not come anywhere near her abuse, Tweety."

"Fuck me, he did that?"

"Yes, she endured years of abuse."

"No, Rem. The shitting on your tits thing."

"No, gross. I didn't *let* him." She shuddered. "He just wanted to. Like I said, way past Christian Grey kinky."

"No shit."

"That was my mandate." She slid my T-shirt up and tugged on it. "I want this off."

"Baby, you're drunk."

"So?"

"Not gonna fuck you when you can't say no."

Her eyes met mine. "I'm not *that* drunk, Tweety. A little over tipsy, but fully coherent. And I would like to suck your cock. You got a problem with that?" She knelt in front of me and unbuttoned my jeans.

"Yeah, baby, I got a problem with that."

"Bullshit," she countered, reaching for my zipper.

I pulled her hands away from my dick and lifted her off the ground.

"Hey!" she growled.

I quieted her by covering her mouth with mine and she slid her hands to my waist.

"Okay, that's good too," she said and smiled against my lips.

"Baby, you need to hydrate."

She ran her tongue over my bottom lip. "I'm good, Tweety."

I cupped her face and tilted her head up. "Remington Charles. You're gonna drink that bottle of water. You get none of my manly bits until you do."

Her button nose wrinkled as she tried to give me a scowl and then she burst out laughing and slid her hands under my now unzipped jeans. "Mmm, I'm gonna have those manly bits even without the water."

"No means no, Remington. I am more than just a sexual being," I said, and put distance between us, snagging the water off the bed.

She giggled. "I know you're more than just a sexual being, Tweety, but not tonight. Tonight, I plan to play with you…all of you."

I held the water out to her. "You're gonna drink this first."

"I'm not a child, Merrick."

"I know that," I said, handing her the water. "Just want to make sure you don't get sick."

She took the water and opened it, drinking deeply before setting it on the table by the window. "Happy now?"

"Yeah, baby, thank you."

"Can I have your manly bits now?"

I spread my arms wide and smiled. "Have at it."

She knelt in front of me and had at it.

* * *

Remington

The shrill ring of my phone drove home the fact I'd drank a little too much and I groaned as I reached to answer it. "Hello?"

"Rem," Kennedy said with a sob. "Chel's in the ICU."

I sat up, rubbing the sleep from my eyes. "What do you mean, she's in the ICU?"

I'd just seen her, and although she looked tired and way too skinny…she'd seemingly lost about twenty pounds in a week…she was upbeat and high on life.

"I had to call the ambulance."

"Oh my god, why?" I cried.

"She—"

"Rem?" Merrick grumbled, cutting off Kennedy's explanation.

"I have to get to the hospital," I said, and threw the covers off. "Where is she, Kennedy? You can fill me in when I get there."

"St. Josephs."

"Okay, I'll be there as soon as I can."

"Okay, honey."

She hung up and I rushed to get dressed, realizing I still didn't have anything clean. "Shit!"

"Baby, what's going on?" Merrick asked and slid out of

the bed.

"Michelle's in the ICU. I need to get to St. Joseph's, but I don't have any fucking clean clothes," I snapped. "And I can't go back to Kennedy's to get anything because she's already at the hospital."

He dragged his hands down his face. "Grab something of mine, honey. I'll take you."

"You don't have to. I'll call for an Uber."

"Remington, you're not calling for an Uber. Get dressed and I'll take you."

"No," I rasped, and dragged one of his T-shirts over my head.

"You're tired and worried, so I'm gonna ignore that," Merrick said, and pulled on his jeans.

"I will get an Uber."

He ignored me and sat down to put on his boots.

"Merrick—"

"You're not getting a fucking Uber, Remington. Just drop it and get dressed."

"What if you're not allowed in?" I challenged.

"Then I'll wait in the waiting room."

"Alone. You'll wait in the waiting room alone."

"Yeah."

"Because you could be stuck there for hours."

"So?"

I burst into tears. "So, you shouldn't have to be stuck in a hospital waiting room alone while I watch my friend die."

"Okay, baby," he said, and rose to his feet, pulling me against his chest. "I'm here whether you want me to be or not. If I have to wait alone in the waiting room, I will."

"Why?"

"Because I love you and you need me."

I wrapped my arms around his waist. "I really do need you," I admitted.

"I know."

"She's dying and there's nothing I can do about it."

"How about we head down to the hospital and see if we can't figure out exactly what's going on, hm?"

I nodded into his chest and then released him, so we could finish dressing and get the fuck out of there.

* * *

We pulled up to the hospital thirty minutes later and headed straight for ICU. We found Kennedy and Michelle's mother, Natalie, in the waiting area and made our way to them. Michelle's dad must be traveling, which didn't surprise me. He was a pilot and not home often.

"Is she okay?" I asked, hugging them both.

"We don't know," Kennedy said. "She came back to my place and collapsed. Heart attack."

"Jebus," I whispered.

"The drugs and chemo were too much for her system. It's why she quit. But it had already done a lot of damage. Her system can't seem to recover, and the drugs aren't helping," Natalie said, rubbing her arms.

Before I could introduce Merrick, a doctor came out to speak to Michelle's mom and we were left standing in the waiting area.

"Are you okay?" I asked Kennedy.

She shook her head. "I thought she was dead," she whispered. "Do you know how hard it is to actually do CPR?"

"No."

"I think I broke her ribs. She's so frail, and I couldn't get her heart to beat."

I wanted to hug her, but Kennedy was not a touchy-feely person. "That must have been terrifying."

I felt Merrick's front hit my back and I leaned back against him as his arm slid around my waist.

"She fell over, Remi. We were talking and laughing and then she was on the floor. It's a miracle she didn't hit her head."

I bit back tears. "I'm sorry I wasn't there, honey."

"There's nothing you could have done," Kennedy said. "The ambulance was there really quickly and the EMT's took over."

"I could have given you moral support."

"That's true," she said.

Natalie walked back to us and smiled. "She's resting comfortably. It was definitely a heart attack, but it was a small one. They're running tests to try and figure out exactly what's going on."

"Can we see her?" I asked.

Natalie shook her head. "She's in isolation to avoid germs. We can't see her for at least forty-eight hours."

"Does she know we're here?" Kennedy asked.

"Yeah, honey, but honestly, the doctor wants us to go home and rest. They will call as soon as she's free for visitors."

"I don't want to leave her," I whispered.

"I'll bring you back the second she's allowed to see you," Merrick promised.

I faced him and met his eyes. "I need to go home with Kennedy."

"Bab—"

"I'm not leaving her alone, honey."

"The problem is, that when I leave you alone, you disappear," he said.

I smiled sadly. "Never again, Tweety. I promise."

"Club get-together tomorrow. You're both coming."

"Can we play it by ear, depending on how Michelle's doing?"

He took a deep breath and stroked my cheek. I could tell he wasn't liking the way this conversation was going.

"Merr, I'm not saying no."

"Wouldn't matter if you were, Rem. No's not an option."

I rolled my eyes. "Okay, Tweety, take it down a notch."

"Want you with me, Rem."

"I know, but you're gonna need to get over it for a day or two."

"Telling me to get over it isn't the way to go here, Rem."

"I don't know what to say here, Merrick. I have to go with Kennedy and I can't be in two places at one time."

He frowned, but then kissed my forehead and nodded. "I get it. I don't like it, but I get it."

"I'm sorry, honey."

"I'll take you both back to Kennedy's."

"Okay."

Merrick made sure Natalie made it to her car safely, then we followed Kennedy to her apartment. The air was heavy in the car, and secretly, my heart was breaking. I didn't want him to leave me at Kennedy's. I wanted to go back to the compound and let him hold me all night. But I also wanted to be with Kennedy. She was the only one who truly understood what I was going through.

We pulled up to a red light and Merrick linked his fingers with mine. I gave his hand a gentle squeeze and tried to smile. I couldn't. I was sad.

Pulling up to Kennedy's place, we climbed out and Merrick insisted on walking us up. Kennedy opened the door and walked inside, but I stood on the porch and wrapped my arms around Merrick.

"Oh, for fuck's sake," Kennedy called out. "Your boy-toy can stay if it'll stop you mooning over him all night."

"No promises," I retorted, and pulled Merrick inside.

Merrick frowned. "I'm not staying if it makes your friend uncomfortable."

"Her friend can speak for herself," Kennedy said from the kitchen. "You're welcome to stay, seriously. You'll have to share the futon or bunk on the floor, but it won't bother me."

"You sure, honey?" I pressed.

"Yeah. I want to drink wine and watch some bad shoot 'em up, so you'll have to deal with that, but it'd be nice to have the company."

I pulled her in for a hug.

"What the fuck are you doing, you weirdo," she said, and broke the hug.

I chuckled. "Just saying thank you."

"Well, do it from twelve inches away from me," she retorted. "Beer or wine, Finch?"

"Beer'd be good. Thanks, Kennedy."

I smiled up at Merrick. "She called you by your super special biker name. She must like you."

"Babe, you're the only person who doesn't. Well, other than my family."

I patted his chest. "I'm in good company, then."

Kennedy returned with a beer for him and a glass of wine for me, and we sat down to watch her shoot 'em up. I ended up falling asleep on Merrick halfway through the movie.

TEN

Remington

I SAT UP with a gasp and found myself pulled onto a warm body. "You okay?" Merrick asked.

I burrowed into him and shook my head. "My friend's dying."

"I know, baby. I got you."

"It's not fair," I whispered. "She's the nicest human being on the planet. Why her? Why can't it be someone like…Vitaly. Jebus, if anyone deserves cancer, it's him."

"No doubt," he said.

"I'm going to hell," I said. "I shouldn't wish cancer on anyone."

"No, I think you're free to wish it on an asshole, degenerate like Vitaly."

"I need her to be okay."

"I know, baby. We're gonna do everything we can."

"Thank you for staying tonight…or today, really."

"You're gonna bring your stuff back to the club, baby, okay? The bed there's more comfortable."

I smiled. "As long as Kennedy's good with it, then yes. The club won't mind?"

"No, baby, they won't mind."

"Now that I have my money back, I should look for a place."

He stiffened. "So you're not coming back with me?"

"I can't leave Michelle, Tweety. Once she's stable, we can talk."

He sighed, giving me a gentle squeeze.

"Okay?" I pressed.

"Yeah."

"Then why do you sound irritated?"

"Because it's not the answer I want to hear," he said.

"It's not the answer I want to give."

"I know."

His phone buzzed on the side table and he reached for it, scowling as he read the screen. "Shit."

"What's wrong?"

"Another body's been found." He put the phone to his ear and sat up. "Hey, Alamo. Yeah, what the fuck? Damn it. Yeah, she's here. Yeah, she's coming back to the compound. Okay. I'll talk to you later."

He hung up and turned to me. "Need to lock you down."

"What does that mean?"

"Another woman's been killed, and threats have been made, so I'm locking you down."

"What kind of threats?"

"The kind that get you, Jasmine, and Willow settled safely at the compound where you'll be guarded by me and my brothers until we find the asshole responsible."

I scrambled up on my knees. "They've threatened us?"

"Yeah."

"By name?"

"Yeah, Rem. By name." He stood and snagged his T-shirt off the floor, pulling it over his head.

"Oh my god. So, he knows us?"

"Apparently."

"What about Kennedy?"

"She wasn't threatened."

"Unless this person is watching me and saw me come here."

"Fuck," he snapped.

"She has to come too," I said.

He pulled out his phone again and fired off a text. "Yeah, baby, she can come too."

"Can we eat first?"

"I'd rather get out of here and eat at the compound."

I climbed off the futon. "I'll go wake Kennedy."

After getting an earful from Kennedy about her need for sleep, she saw reason, and packed a bag, finally agreeing to come with us. Mostly because she said she was horny and being in a building with a 'shit ton of hot bikers' might assuage that horniness.

I rolled my eyes and made my way back out to the living room. I didn't really care why she was coming with us, just that she was.

After loading our bags into Merrick's rental, we headed back to the compound…although, Kennedy insisted on following us.

"Are they going to let Kennedy in?" I asked.

"Who?"

"The badass biker brigade."

Merrick glanced at me. "The badass biker brigade?"

"You know…the guards."

He chuckled. "Yeah, baby, they'll let her in."

"Why are you laughing at me?"

"Because you're adorable and you amuse me."

"Excuse me?" I said, shifting to face him. "I *amuse*

you."

"*All* the time." He took my hand and gave it a squeeze. "I love your view on my world, Rem. It's refreshing and funny, and…adorable."

"You're lucky you're good with your mouth or I'd take offense at your patronizing tone."

He laughed and released my hand as we pulled up to the compound gates. "Gonna show you just how patronizing I can be later…and I'm gonna use more than my mouth. That I can promise you."

I shivered with anticipation while he spoke with Stump about letting Kennedy through and then we were inside the compound gates and I found myself relaxing.

"You okay?" Merrick asked.

I nodded. "I didn't realize I was on edge, to be honest, until we drove in." I leaned forward to kiss him gently. "Thanks for always making me feel safe."

He smiled. "You're welcome."

"I love you."

"Love you back."

We climbed out of the car, grabbed our stuff, then led Kennedy inside. We walked in to find Jasmine and the rest of the 'old ladies,' already putting a dent in a bottle or two of wine.

"I'm gonna drop your stuff off, then we got a meeting," Merrick said. "You good hangin' with the women?"

"Yeah, honey, I'm good. I plan on drinking a lot, just so you know."

He squeezed my chin gently. "Not too much, okay? I want you lucid."

I bit my lip and nodded. "I'll be lucid."

"Good." He leaned down and kissed me, then left the room and I joined the women. Quin was sitting on the floor, playing with the cutest little girl I'd ever seen.

"Kinsey, honey, can I sit on the sofa now?" Quin asked.

"No, Mama, it's wava."

"I thought the coffee table was lava."

Kinsey took a deep breath, placed her hands on each of Quin's cheeks and shook her head. "You're not wistening, Mama."

"Oh, sorry," Quin said and put on a serious face. "Tell me again."

I bit back a smile as I watched the exchange. Kinsey was apparently very good at schooling Quin on how lava worked.

"Wine?" Jasmine asked, and I nodded.

"Got beer?" Kennedy asked.

"Kitchen," Jasmine said. "Help yourself."

As Kennedy headed to the kitchen, a tall, gorgeous blond man walked in the room with a just as gorgeous dark-haired man and Kinsey no longer cared about Quin or the lava. She made a run for the blond who scooped her up above his head and grinned. "Hey, princess, how's my girl?"

"Mama's on wava."

"Jesus." Quin dropped her head back with a dramatic groan, hauling herself off the floor. "I thought the sofa was lava."

I deduced this was Badger, which meant the other man was Dash. I hadn't met them yet, but Merrick had filled me in on who everyone was attached to…sort of.

Willow raised her head as Dash kissed her upside down. "You good?"

"We've been here for less than an hour, how un-good could I get in that time?" she retorted, then grinned. "But I love you for checking in."

Kennedy walked back over to me holding a beer and sat on the sofa.

"Have you met Remington and Kennedy yet?" Willow asked Dash.

Dash raised his head and gave us a chin lift. "Nice to meet you."

"You too," I said at the same time Kennedy did.

Merrick and Alamo arrived, and Merrick made his way to me, lowering himself onto the couch and wrapping an arm around my shoulder.

"You can't be done, right?"

"Nah. Doc's dealing with something so we figured we'd order pizza while he's working."

I smiled. "Pizza sounds amazing."

He chuckled. "I love how much you love food."

"Well, I don't get to eat like this when I'm dancing, so I'm taking advantage."

"I like what it does for your ass," he whispered.

"Stop," I ordered.

He buried his face in my neck and I shivered. "Stop what?"

"Tweety," I warned.

"Yeah, baby?"

I faced him with a frown. "Stop, or you're going to have to take me somewhere—"

"We got time," he interrupted.

"Finch," Alamo called.

"I jinxed it," he said, and kissed me before standing. "Yeah, man."

I watched him walk toward the men…well, I watched his ass walk that way. Merrick had an incredible ass, then they headed to the kitchen, Badger still carrying Kinsey.

"I kind of wish my kid wasn't so smart," Quin complained, flopping onto the sofa. "She's way too much like her daddy."

I was confused by that statement, because Michael was kind of a creep, and I knew Quin was divorcing him, so it seemed weird that she'd say something somewhat positive about him.

"If you're not here in twenty minutes, Liv, I'm gonna fuckin' collect you myself," Doc growled into his phone as he walked through the great room.

I raised an eyebrow and Jasmine rolled her eyes, while Willow covered her mouth hiding a laugh.

"Don't give a fuck," he continued, "You've got nineteen minutes now."

I couldn't tear my eyes away. His body was locked, his face was contorted in irritation, but he also looked like he was enjoying her side of the conversation a little more than might be normal.

"Olivia," he said, slowly. "Either you're here in eighteen minutes or I'll send Stump to pick you up." He shook his head. "No, me gettin' you is now off the table. Yeah, I *can* make that call, 'cause I'm the fuckin' president of this chapter." He cocked his head. "Oh, you don't think so? Get your pretty ass down here, baby. I'm hangin' up now."

He hung up and then seemed to notice we were there watching him. He grinned his signature charming smile. "Ladies."

"Hey, Doc," Jasmine said. "Everything okay?"

"Golden, babe," he said, then nodded and walked toward the kitchen.

Willow finally let her laughter go and Jasmine grinned and took a sip of wine.

"What was that all about?" I asked.

"Olivia won't give him the time of day," Jasmine said.

"Well, that's not entirely true," Willow countered.

"Oh, she'll give him her pussy on occasion, but nothing else and it's driving him insane," Quin said.

"Quin," Willow admonished. "It sounds like you're slut shaming her."

"Not at all," she argued. "He's just way more into her than she is him."

Jasmine snorted. "Don't think that's true."

"Why not?" I asked.

"Because she's in love with him."

"No she's not," Quin said.

"She so is," Willow countered.

"Then why is she so cold to Doc?"

"Gee, Quin, I don't know," Jasmine deadpanned. "Why is she so cold to Doc?"

Quin rolled her eyes. "Oh, *please*. I am not cold to Knox."

"Who's Knox?" I asked.

"Badger," Willow provided.

"Ah," I said.

"You feel free to live your fantasy," Jasmine said.

"It's complicated," Quin said.

"I don't doubt that," Kennedy piped in.

Doc stalked back through the room looking ready to kill, and my focus was pulled to him again. I sipped my wine and sat back to watch the show that was sure to come.

"Stump!" Doc bellowed outside.

I knew for a fact Stump was watching the gate, so Doc had to yell for him again.

"Oh, shit, it's about to get real," Kennedy murmured.

There was silence for several minutes and then a very frazzled, very pissed off looking woman stomped into the room, dropping a duffel bag on the floor.

"Goddammit, Liv," Doc snapped, following her.

"I'm here," she growled out. "What more do you want, Tristan?"

"I swear to Christ, I'll—"

"What? What will you do, Tris?" she challenged. "Huh? I'm here."

"You're late."

"I'm here!" she snapped.

He scowled at her for a few more seconds, then turned on his heel and left the room. Olivia grabbed the bottle of wine on the table and took a long pull from it, forgoing a glass.

"You okay?" Jasmine asked.

"Murder's still illegal, right?"

"Yes, but I'm here for you if you need to hide a body."

"Not a hair, not a fiber, Jazz," Olivia said.

"Oh, I know how to deal with hair," Jazz assured, and they burst into giggles.

I made a mental note not to piss these women off as I focused on my wine.

"Liv," Doc called.

She craned her neck, but didn't get off the couch. "Yeah?"

"Got a minute?"

"Do I look like I 'got a minute'?"

"Babe," he breathed out.

"Jesus, Doc, keep your pants on," she hissed out, handing the wine to Jasmine and standing. "I'll be right back."

I had a clear view of the couple as Doc slid his hand to her neck and then guided her through the kitchen.

"He's so fucking gone for her," Quin said.

"Looks like she feels the same," Kennedy said. "She's just protesting too much."

I had a feeling my bestie was right, but I didn't say that out loud.

ELEVEN

Finch

WALKED INTO the meeting room and sat beside Dash who gave me a chin lift. "How long are you here?"

"Couple of weeks," I said. "Gotta get Remington sorted, then get back to Portland."

"We should go out. The four of us."

"I'm in," I said, just as Doc walked in.

"Thanks for getting here so quickly," Doc said, and took his place at the head of the table.

Today we were meeting in the room utilized for church. The large mahogany table had a glass top with the Dogs of Fire flag between it, along with the patches of dead club members.

I knew I'd been invited in only because Remington was one of the ones threatened, and I didn't take that for granted, but I also wasn't gonna sit back and stay quiet if it meant Remington was exposed.

"We've got a lot of shit to cover, so I'll get right to it," Doc continued. "I got a call from Dalton Moore, who let me know the F.B.I. have arrested a suspect in the Gentleman Strangler case."

The room began to celebrate, but Doc quickly cut us off.

"Shut the fuck up, all of you. There's more news, none of it's good, and it involves everyone in this room. More importantly, it involves our women."

"What the fuck are you talking about?" I asked. "Is there more going on than verbal threats?"

"Verbal threats with some serious money behind them," Doc clarified. "The guy the F.B.I.'s picked up is Seth Backstrom."

"Backstrom. Why does that name sound familiar?" Doom asked. Doom was the road captain for the club and had some serious anger issues. No one crossed him. Ever.

"Because the Backstrom family is related to the Ellis family, and they're about as rich and powerful as it gets," Alamo said. "In fact, Seth Backstrom is Thomas Ellis's cousin."

"What the fuck?" I snapped.

"That's right," Doc said. "They share a grandmother. Seth lives in North Carolina now, but he and Thomas grew up together, about as close as brothers could be, and would spend every summer at their grandparents' property in Savannah. The F.B.I. are currently working off the theory that Thomas and Seth have been in this together all along, and that Thomas's death has triggered these recent killings."

"What's Seth saying?" I asked.

"Not much, considering." Doc and Alamo shared a look.

I frowned. "Considering what?"

"Local PD pulled Seth over for a busted taillight and the officer noticed he was acting strange. He was evasive and didn't want to answer even simple questions. The officer asked him to step out of the car and that's when he went from quiet to stone silent. The officer said Seth was like a robot, and someone had thrown his standby switch. Seth refused to acknowledge the officer's commands or comply with his requests, so he took him to county figuring he was high on drugs. He was searched and placed in a private holding cell, but the guard who processed him missed the razor blade hidden in the waistband of his underwear. Before he could be questioned, he cut out his own tongue."

"Jesus," I hissed.

"The guard said Seth was sitting perfectly still on his bunk, hands folded, with his tongue in his lap. The only indication he'd butchered himself was the copious amount of blood all over his front. He never made a noise, no cry of pain, nothing. He was rushed to county hospital, and it was then that they started carefully going through his belongings, which is why the F.B.I. was notified."

"What the fuck did they find?" Doom asked.

"Among his belongings was a small notebook full of poetry."

"Poetry?" I asked.

Doc nodded. "Yeah, really dark and twisted shit. It's all violent and it's all about three women. Women he refers to as the Flower, the Tree, and the Gun. The poetry is all about what he's going to do to these women when he gets his hands on them. How he'll dress them and strangle them before taking their photos."

"Sounds familiar," Alamo said.

"Exactly, so the police notified the F.B.I., but before they arrived, Seth decided to plead the fifth permanently."

"So, if the Feds think this guy and Thomas were working together, why the cause for alarm if they've got him? Why the lockdown?"

"The F.B.I. analysts had no idea who the Flower, Tree, and Gun could be, but as soon as Agent Moore saw the poetry, and the connection had been made between Seth and Thomas, he knew who they were."

"Who are they?" I asked.

"Think about it. If he's upset about Thomas's killing, wouldn't it make sense that he'd make the Dogs of Fire pay? And if he kills women, wouldn't it stand to reason that he'd come after ours? Jasmine is the Flower, Willow the Tree, and Remington…"

"The Gun," I said.

"Holy shit," Doom said.

"Exactly, so we're not taking any chances. We're gonna make sure we've got protection for every single one of our women. Just because he only mentioned three, doesn't mean we know what he has planned, and we sure as hell don't know if he and Thomas were the only ones involved." He turned to Doom. "You got Aspen secure?"

Doom nodded.

"This just keeps getting better," Badger ground out.

"In addition to bringing everyone here that we can, I also want Stump to guard Michelle's hospital room and I want soldiers posted at every officer's house. Seth is hiding a big fucking secret and we're not gonna be surprised by it when the time comes."

Everyone in the room nodded, and we discussed the logistics of the protection details for the next half-hour before breaking.

* * *

Remington

Soft lips on mine had me smiling as I forced my eyes open. "I thought you said you'd be lucid," Merrick accused.

"I was just resting so I'd be ready for you."

He chuckled, pulling me up off the sofa gently. "Let's head to bed."

"Wait, where's Kennedy?" I asked.

"She's been taken care of."

"Meaning?"

"Let's just say that sometimes the cheese gets the Mouse."

I frowned. "Huh?"

"Don't wor—"

I gasped. "Oh my god, she's bumping uglies with that really young guy? The one you call Mouse?"

"I'm not sure what they're doing, but they headed off toward an empty bunkroom, so I can deduce that, yeah."

"Is he nice?"

"Don't know him, but from what Alamo says, he's a good guy, baby."

"You checked?"

"Yeah."

"To make sure she was safe?"

He smiled. "Yeah."

"God, I love you," I whispered, and kissed him.

"Love you, too." He took my hand and gave it a squeeze. "Let's hit the hay."

"I should get my stuff."

"Already sorted, Rem."

"Maybe I should fall asleep on the sofa more often."

Merrick chuckled and led me upstairs, pushing open his door and stepping back. I walked in, flipping on the light as I passed the switch, then turning to face him.

"How did your meeting go?"

He shook his head.

"Not good?"

"I'm not talking about it."

I wrinkled my nose. "So it was bad."

"Remington, I'm not talking about it."

"Well, are you up to fucking me? Hard?"

"Has there *ever* been a moment when I wasn't up to fucking you…hard?"

I smiled. "Just want to make sure, honey. If you've had

a difficult meeting, I don't want to add stress to you."

"I know what you're doing."

I slid my hands under his shirt. "What am I doing?"

"You're trying to get me to talk about the meeting."

"Fine." I sighed, sliding my hand under his shirt. "If you don't want to talk, then you need to fuck me."

He chuckled. "That I can do."

Sliding off his cut, he pulled his T-shirt off and I felt the need to run my tongue over his Dogs of Fire tattoo. Tugging at the waistband of his jeans, I unbuttoned them and pushed them down his hips, his dick springing free as I knelt in front of him.

He stroked my cheek. "I thought I was fucking *you*."

"After I blow you."

"Oh, yeah?"

I ran my tongue up his length. "Yeah."

I wrapped my lips around the head of his cock, taking his length as deep as I could, working the shaft with my hand, and jacking him with the same motion of my mouth.

Merrick's hand went to the crown of my head and his fingers dug into my scalp. I knew he was close to coming when his fingers squeezed a little harder. "Rem."

I cupped his balls and took him deeper, jacking just a little faster.

"Fuck, Rem." His hand twitched again. "Now, baby."

I sucked a little harder and he came. Hard. I took every ounce down my throat, then felt myself lifted and dropped onto the bed where my clothes were practically ripped from my body.

Then his mouth was on my pussy and I was writhing against him, trying to figure out a way to hold off my orgasm.

I never found one.

Instead, I came so hard and so fast, I could barely catch my breath, but then Merrick shifted me onto my stomach and lifted my hips, sliding into me and he was building yet another orgasm in me.

Merrick slammed into me. Flesh slapped against flesh as our bodies connected, and an orgasm hovered at the edge. I wanted to come… wanted it more than anything, but I needed this to last. Goosebumps swept across my skin and I knew I wouldn't be able to wait much longer. "Merrick," I begged.

"Wait."

"Baby, I can't."

"Wait, Remington."

I whimpered as his hand connected with my ass, and I forced myself to hold back, but when his palm connected again, I lost my composure.

"Merrick!" I screamed as I came, my pussy contracting around his cock.

He thrust again, then once more, his hand connecting with my bare flesh with a smack, and I cried out as another orgasm hit.

He wasn't far behind and we fell into a heap of sweat and heavy breathing, his arms coming around me and holding me tight. "I love you, Remington."

"I love you too, honey."

"Want you to marry me, baby."

I gasped, rolling to face him. "What?"

"Want to make this permanent."

"Tweety, we've barely known each other a week."

"Two years and a week," he countered.

"You don't think this is a little rash?"

"Nope."

"We don't know each other."

"I'm not saying we have to get married tomorrow. Just want to make it a little more permanent."

"Are you going to stay here with me?"

"I can't. I was hoping you'd come home with me."

"I can't, Merrick."

He sighed. "Then we'll need to figure some shit out."

"Which is why we can't get married."

"Oh, we're getting married, Remington. Have no doubt about that."

"I haven't said yes, Tweety."

"You will," he said, and kissed me gently before sliding off the bed and heading to the bathroom.

I followed him. "I don't think we'll ever make this work."

He disposed of the condom. "I know, Eeyore."

"I'm not being Eeyore about this, Merrick. We live on opposite sides of the country. I don't think I could make a long-distance thing work."

He smiled, then washed his hands and face, totally ignoring my comment.

"Fuck you, Merrick," I snapped and stomped back into his bedroom.

His arm snaked around me and his face burrowed into my neck. "Baby."

"No. You don't get to minimize this."

"I'm not."

"Yes, you are," I argued. "We have a real hurdle here. Not something small or insignificant."

"I know, honey. We'll figure it out."

I turned in his arms and frowned up at him. "How?"

"I don't know yet, but are you willing to figure it out with me?"

I shrugged, tracing my finger over his collarbone.

"Is that a yes or a no?"

I shrugged again.

"Remington, are you being difficult?"

"I don't know, Tweety, am I?"

His lips twitched, and I forced myself not to smile. "Fuck me, you're gorgeous."

"Even when I'm being difficult?"

"*Especially* when you're being difficult," he whispered, and kissed me.

Before things could get interesting, his phone buzzed on the nightstand, and he answered it without looking at the screen, then scowled. "Hey." He glanced at me. "Yeah, sissy. Yep." He handed the phone to me. "My sister wants a word."

I bit my lip. "Should I be scared?" I whispered.

"Probably."

I took his phone and said, "Hey, Grace."

"Are you fucking kidding me? 'Hey, Grace.' Is that all you have to say?"

"Well—"

"You disappeared. Not cool. In fact, it was a total twat thing to do."

"Well—"

"I'm not finished."

I bit my lip again and stared at Merrick in desperation. He just shook his head and shrugged.

"We are friends, are we not?"

"Of course we are," I said.

"Okay, well, my friends don't disappear without saying goodbye."

"I'm sorry, Grace."

"I don't accept," she snapped. "Not yet, anyway."

"Ah…"

"You don't get to do that again, Remington. I need you to hear me on that. I will put up with a lot of shit, but if we're friends, you don't get to just fuck off and worry me. It's not cool, Rem."

No, I couldn't imagine it would be with everything she'd gone through.

"I know, honey. I really am sorry. From the bottom of my heart."

"I don't want you to apologize, Remi, I want you to never do it again."

"I promise, I'll never do it again."

"Prove it."

"I will, Grace."

"Okay. You can give the phone back to my brother."

I handed the phone back to Merrick, then stepped into the bathroom. I'd fucked up with Grace, and I didn't realize how much until Merrick had filled me in on her trauma. I was a bitch. Now, I just had to figure out how to make it up to her.

"You okay?"

I continued to stare at the sink as I shook my head. "I fucked up, Tweety."

"You didn't fuck up. Erred slightly, but Grace'll forgive you. She probably already has."

I washed my hands, still focusing on the sink, but as I rinsed, the faucet was turned off and I was turned toward Merrick. "You're safe, honey."

"I know."

"Do you?"

I nodded. "Yes."

"Emotionally."

I dropped my eyes. "Oh."

"Oh," he mimicked, lifting my chin and meeting my eyes again. "You're safe in that regard too."

"I'm starting to get that, Tweety."

"Yeah?"

"Yes. I'm just not used to it."

"I get it."

"What happened in the meeting?" I asked.

He sighed.

"You don't have to tell me everything, Merrick. But I *am* the one being threatened, so I feel I have the right to know something."

"Do you know Seth Backstrom?"

"He's Thomas's cousin. I met him a couple of times, why?"

"He's the one who issued the threats."

I gasped. "Why?"

"Pretty sure he's deep in Thomas's pockets. Or he was when he was alive."

I nodded. "That makes sense, and they were really close, but he was nice. I can't imagine him making threats, let alone murdering anyone."

"Well, he did, baby, so don't minimize this."

"I'm not," I said, and frowned up at him. "What aren't you telling me?"

"Something I have no intention of telling you."

"Because you don't trust me?"

He ran a finger down my cheek. "Because I'm not putting the visual in your head."

"It's bad?" I asked.

"It's worse than bad, Rem," he said. "We've got people watching Michelle."

"Jebus, that *is* bad."

"Yeah."

"Kennedy's going to freak."

"She's covered."

I shook my head. "No. She dated Seth."

"Fuck me."

"Later," I retorted. "Focus on this right now."

His lips twitched, and he kissed me gently. "I need to let Doc know about Kennedy. He'll want to talk to her."

"You're really going to leave me right now?"

"I don't need to nowadays, baby," he said in a thick old tyme, southern accent. "We got these things, they're texting machines, and I can even make what these newfangled folks call a phone call."

I rolled my eyes. "You're a butt."

He grinned and snagged his phone off the nightstand, firing off a text. "Done."

I bit back a yawn. "I'm going to text Michelle's mom, then can we sleep?"

"Yeah, baby, we can."

I nodded, digging my phone out of my purse and sending a quick text. Her mom texted back that there still wasn't any news, so I curled up against Merrick and quickly fell asleep.

TWELVE

Remington

THE PEAL OF my phone broke through my restful sleep and I groaned as I grabbed it off the nightstand. "Hello?"

Sobbing came through and I sat up.

"Rem?" she said on a hiccup.

"Natalie?"

"Honey, she's gone."

"Who's gone?"

"Michelle."

"Gone where?" I asked, still not completely awake.

"Honey, she's dead."

"What?" I squeaked, and Merrick's arm wrapped around my waist. "How?"

"Her heart stopped again, and they couldn't get it started again."

"No." I slid off the bed and made my way to my bag. "They have to keep trying. She'll come back. Zap her or something."

"Honey, they did everything they could. The chemo was too much. Her body couldn't handle it anymore."

"Are you at the hospital?" I asked. "I'll come and talk to the doctor."

"Yes, I'm here, but, honestly, sweetness, you don't want to be here."

"I'm coming right now. I'll wake Kennedy."

"No, honey, please don't."

Before I could argue, my phone was pulled from my hand and Merrick took over. "Natalie? Hey, it's Finch. What do you need?"

I huffed. "She needs to get the doctor—"

Merrick held his hand up and shook his head. When I opened my mouth to argue, he walked into the bathroom. "Yeah, Natalie, we can do that." I followed, but he walked back into the bedroom before I got to him. "Yeah, sweetheart, we got you. Okay. We'll see you tomorrow."

Hanging up, he dropped my phone on the bed and closed the distance between us. I sidestepped him as I pulled a T-shirt over my head and grabbed my jeans off the floor.

"Rem, we're not leaving here tonight."

"You might not be, but I am."

He wrapped an arm around my waist and anchored me to his body. "No. You're. Not."

"Let me go."

"No."

"I have to tell the doctors to try again."

"Honey, she's gone."

I shook my head. "Let me go."

"I'm here, Rem. I got you."

"She's not dead," I whispered. "She can't be gone."

His arms wrapped around me like a gentle vice and he

stroked my back. That's when I lost my shit…on his chest. In the form of my fists. He let me go for a few seconds before grabbing my wrists and pulling my arms behind me and I dropped my face in his chest and sobbed. He somehow guessed my legs couldn't hold me and slid his arm under my knees, lifting me onto the bed and stretching us out so he could pull me into his arms.

"I'm here, baby."

"She can't be dead. She can't. She was supposed to fight."

"She did fight, honey."

"I need more time. I still have to do the swab thing. Have them take my blood, save her life."

"We'll do the swab thing in her name, honey. Save someone else."

"I don't want to save someone else. I want Michelle back."

A loud bang sounded on the door, then Kennedy bellowed, "Remi, open the door."

Merrick slid off the bed and pulled on a pair of jeans, while I wrapped a sheet around me. He yanked open the door and Kennedy rushed in. Mouse stayed in the hallway while Kennedy wrapped me in a hug. "Did you hear?"

"Yeah, honey, Natalie called."

"She won't let us go down to the hospital."

I sighed. "I know."

"What the fuck, Remi?"

"We'll take you down tomorrow," Merrick said.

"I want to go down there tonight," Kennedy snapped.

"I think Michelle's parents need some time alone with her," I said. "We should give them that, honey."

"Why the hell is she dead?" Kennedy whispered.

I wrapped my arms around her. "I don't know. It sucks."

"Kennedy," Mouse said from the threshold. "Come get some rest, we'll head to the hospital tomorrow."

"Fucked you once, buddy, doesn't mean you get to boss me around."

He chuckled. "Funny you think that. Come on, baby."

She rolled her eyes, hugged me again, then left me alone with Merrick.

"I need alcohol," I admitted.

"What ya want?" Merrick asked.

"Amaretto sours. Lots of them."

"You wanna come with me or stay here?"

I leaned against him, squeezing his arm. "Come with you. Does that sound super needy?"

"So fuckin' needy, baby," he deadpanned. "We'll get you tipsy enough to sleep and we can discuss you getting some therapy when you wake up."

"I love how willing you are to take care of me."

"It's my life's goal. I'm in service of the queen."

I smiled sadly up at him. "I like the sound of that."

He stroked my cheek. "You're gonna get through this, honey. I'm here."

I blinked back tears and nodded. "Thanks, Tweety."

He kissed me gently, then we headed downstairs to find booze.

* * *

The next morning, I awoke to discover a voicemail from Natalie. I couldn't believe I'd slept through my phone ringing, but I'd drunk enough to make me forget for a little while, so that meant I'd drunk enough to sleep through the rest of the night without waking.

"Hi, honey. Michelle is headed to Shady Pines Funeral home. If you and Kennedy want to meet me there at four this afternoon, you can spend some time with her before they get her ready for cremation. If you can't make it, that's absolutely okay. Just let me know."

She hung up and I flopped back onto the bed.

"Bad news?" Merrick asked as he pulled me over his

chest.

"Kennedy and I can go down to the funeral home at four. She's going to be cremated, but Michelle always wanted to donate."

"She might not qualify now if her heart's destroyed."

"True."

"Mom wanted to do the same thing, but she kind of blew her head off. They didn't get to her fast enough, so…"

"Oh, god," I whispered, hugging him tight.

"She was far too damaged, so Dad had her cremated as well."

"I'm so sorry you had to deal with that."

"Yeah, it fucking sucked."

"I don't doubt it." I kissed him just over his Dogs of Fire tattoo. "I love you."

"Love you back."

"You don't need to come with me today. Kennedy and I can go."

"You seriously think you're going anywhere alone right now?"

"No. I just wanted to give you an out."

"I don't want a fucking out," he ground out. "I'm driving you."

I nodded against his chest. "Thanks, honey."

"You're welcome." He gave me a gentle squeeze. "How are you feeling?"

"Not bad, surprisingly." I smiled up at him. "The water and ibuprofen helped."

"Good," he said.

It hadn't been lost on me that Merrick had watched me like a hawk as I drank one amaretto sour after another, then foregoing the sour, making sure I drank water in between each new beverage. He'd virtually carried me up to his room before making sure I took ibuprofen before we fell into bed. He'd tended to both my physical and emotional needs, as I was realizing he always did.

"You always take care of me," I whispered.

He kissed my temple. "I was serious when I said I'm in service of the queen."

"I'm letting that sink in, honey."

"Fuckin' finally," he breathed out.

I rolled my eyes even as I snuggled closer.

"You hungry?"

"Starved," I admitted.

"Want your man to make you breakfast?"

"Is bacon on the table?"

"Bacon's *always* on the table," he said.

"Then, yes, I'd like my man to make me breakfast."

He kissed me gently, then slid out of bed and pulled on his jeans and a T-shirt.

* * *

I gripped Merrick's hand as we walked into the funeral home. Kennedy walked with us, her shoulders drooped, her defeated countenance so unlike her normal self. She refused to let Mouse come with her, making it clear (again) he was a one-night stand and it would never be more than that. I had to give it to Mouse, he took it like a man and didn't seem to let her rejection faze him.

We were met by Mr. Lamb, who was an older man, balding and thin, with a calm and gentle demeanor. "I am so sorry for your loss."

"Thank you," I said.

"Michelle's parents are with her now. Will you follow me?"

I nodded, and Kennedy led the way, following Mr. Lamb.

"Whatever you need, Rem," Merrick whispered as we were ushered to where Michelle was waiting.

Natalie sat between her husband, Don, and son, Gabriel, and turned with a sad smile as Kennedy and I walked in.

I hadn't seen Michelle's dad, Don, in ages, but now he sat with his arm tight around Natalie and he looked wrecked. Understandably. Michelle was their only daughter and she'd always been a daddy's girl.

Gabe and I were friends. Not like Michelle and I were friends, but he and his sister were close, so he was often at the same parties, bars, clubs, and get-togethers we frequented. If he'd had a vagina, he would have been the fourth in our group.

We made our way to them and they stood and hugged us tight, Gabe holding me a little longer than the rest, then they hung back and I walked with Kennedy up the three stairs to where Michelle was lying in a very simple but elegant casket.

Kennedy took my hand and squeezed, then reached in and fixed Michelle's collar. "She has to look her best."

"Very true," I agreed as tears poured down my face.

Michelle used to joke that she wanted no hair out of place, even when she started losing it. She'd made the decision to shave her head the second her hair started falling out. I stroked her cheek, her skin so pale and soft it felt as thin as paper, but even in death she was beautiful.

All such a waste.

Strong arms wrapped around me from behind as I crumpled, and Merrick carried me to a row of chairs next to Gabe, settling me on his lap as he sat down. I wanted to be strong. I wanted to stop crying, because I was a friend who had lost a friend, but Don and Natalie had lost their *child*. But I couldn't get a grip on my emotions and I sobbed uncontrollably into Merrick's neck.

It was real…all way too real. My best friend was dead. There was no way to bring her back and I was instantly lost.

"It's okay, honey," Natalie crooned, rubbing my back. "Let it out."

"I'm so…sorry…Natalie. I didn't…want to cry."

"Oh, baby, it's okay to cry."

"But she was your daughter. It's sadder for you," I rasped.

"Sweetness, I know how y'all feel about each other. You were…*are* sisters. It's sad, so be sad. Your pain is no less real than mine. It's okay."

I nodded into Merrick's chest, letting the sadness swamp me. Kennedy sat beside Natalie and they held each other as Michelle's dad left the room. He was a stoic man, so that didn't surprise me, but it did make me cry a little harder.

Merrick stroked my hair and pulled me closer as I wept into his shirt. I couldn't seem to stop, the loss so intense, the pain so visceral. I didn't know what I was going to do without her. I didn't know what the world was going to do without her.

I don't know how long we sat there, him holding me, Natalie and Kennedy holding each other, but the lights in the room came on, so I figured it was probably getting dark outside.

I'd stopped crying, but continued to burrow into the warmth and safety of Merrick's body. Mr. Lamb cleared his throat and Natalie nodded, rising to her feet. "We should go. You can both come back tomorrow if you like. She'll be cremated on Monday, then we'll work on a memorial service."

"I can help with that," I said.

"Me too," Kennedy agreed.

"Thank you. We'll really need your input."

Don had come back into the room a while ago, but he hadn't said a thing. He still didn't as he hugged me tight, kissing the top of my head, doing the same to Kennedy.

"Remi, you got a second?" Gabe asked, and I nodded, pulling away from Merrick.

Gabe slid his arm around my shoulders and led me off to the side of the room, out of earshot of the group. He pulled me in for a hug and I couldn't stop myself from glancing at Merrick whose body had just locked, as his gaze hyper-focused on Gabe. I pulled away from my friend, but let him keep hold of my hand.

"Who's the guy, Rem?"

"Merrick. I met him a couple of years ago."

"A biker."

"A lawyer."

"He's a fuckin' lawyer *and* a biker?" Gabe asked, his tone one of disgust.

"Yeah." I pulled my hand away and crossed my arms. "And I love him, so how about you stow your attitude?"

"Don't like that you're with some biker gang."

"Oh my god, Gabe, I'm not with a biker gang," I snapped. He was acting like a jealous boyfriend and I wanted nothing to do with it. "I can't believe you're pulling all this shit in front of your parents, at Michelle's viewing. It's totally inappropriate, not to mention, *none* of your business."

"Time to go," Merrick said, stepping between me and Gabe and taking my hand. He stood facing Gabe, which meant, I was hidden and protected…like always.

"Excuse me, I was speaking with Remington."

"And now you're done," Merrick said.

"I beg to differ."

"Don't give a fuck. You wanna talk to Remington, you call or text and set up a more appropriate time. But, you're on notice. If you plan to lay into her like you're doing right now, you're not getting anywhere near her."

"You her guard dog?"

"Yeah, you could say that," Merrick retorted.

"Gabe, text me, okay?" I said, gripping Merrick's arm with my free hand. Our fingers were still linked, and I held on tight, taking his support. "Maybe we can get together after the memorial service. Sound good?"

"We're leaving now," Kennedy announced, glaring at

Gabe. She'd never been the biggest fan of Michelle's brother, but that was probably because she'd hit it and quit it, and broke his heart a little. He hadn't handled it well, and made her life difficult whenever he could, which made Kennedy rage a little.

Merrick wrapped his arm around my waist, gave Gabe a chin lift, then walked me and Kennedy out to the lobby where several of the Dogs were waiting…including Mouse.

Kennedy made a beeline for him, falling against him as his arms wrapped around her like a vice. This was interesting…and weird. Kennedy said she only believed in one-night stands. She wasn't relationship material and refused to be tied down. I was getting the impression her opinion may be changing on that front.

Merrick took my hand again, and a few of the bikers gathered around and formed a protective circle as we stepped outside. Once inside the car, I noticed Kennedy didn't follow.

"Mouse has her," Merrick explained. "We'll head back to the compound and you can get drunk with everyone or we can hang in my room."

"I don't want to see anyone."

"Okay, baby, we don't have to see anyone."

"You can hang with your brothers, honey. I'll be okay."

"If you think I'm leaving you alone, you're high."

I smiled. "Thanks, Tweety."

He linked his fingers with mine. "You're welcome, Ee-yore."

Arriving back at the compound, we parked toward the back of the property, considering the parking areas were packed with bikes and family cars. I really didn't want to see anyone, but I didn't need to worry, Merrick guided me in the back and up a different set of stairs, away from the crowd. I knew Kennedy would be tended to, so I let Merrick take me to his room and I curled up on the newly made bed, hugging a pillow to my chest.

"I'm gonna go grab food," Merrick said, kissing my cheek. "I won't be long."

"Okay," I whispered.

"Text me if you have a craving."

"Pickles and ice cream."

"Okay, baby."

"And wine."

"Got it."

"Burger," I said.

He chuckled. "I'm going, honey. Text me if you want more."

I nodded, and he headed out.

* * *

I woke to an empty bed. A little discombobulated as to where I was, it took me a second to realize I was in only my panties and tucked into Merrick's bed.

I sat up and reached for the lamp on the nightstand, flipping it on and finding a note sitting underneath.

Downstairs, baby. Text me if I'm not next to you. Tweety.

I noticed Merrick had plugged my phone in and set it next to the note, so I sent him a quick text to let him know I was awake, then headed to the bathroom.

"Rem?" Merrick called, apparently having flown up the stairs.

"Bathroom," I called back as I washed my hands.

"You okay?" he asked from the doorway.

"I don't like waking up and finding you not next to me," I said and dried my hands. "But other than that, I'm good."

He held his arm out and I walked into his hug. "I was saying hi to a couple people. Sorry I wasn't here."

I smiled up at him and kissed his neck. "I'm just giving you a hard time. I'm good, honey. Love that you signed the note with Tweety."

"Yeah?"

"Yep."

"You hungry?"

"Starved." I fell asleep before I could eat, so I was now ravenous, and everything sounded good to me.

"I brought up a few things, but I can run down and grab you a burger if you want."

I nodded. "That would be amazing."

"Yeah?"

"I'm hungry enough to eat an entire cow, so, yeah."

He kissed me gently, then left me again. I took a few minutes to pull on one of his T-shirts and pull my hair back in a scrunchy before he returned with a burger and potato salad, along with a carton of ice cream and a bottle of my favorite wine.

"Do you want to go back down to the party?" I asked, then took a bite of the burger.

"Nah, I'm good, baby. I'm all yours."

"You sure you don't have anyone else you need to catch up with?"

"Pretty sure I'm covered. Why?"

"Because I'm gonna eat, then I'm gonna brush my teeth because I love you, you're welcome, then you're gonna fuck me. Hard." I smiled and forked some potato salad into my mouth as I focused on Merrick's dick. The fact it rose to attention at my promise made me eat a little faster and by the time I'd brushed my teeth and slid out of his T-shirt, Merrick had me on the bed and was yanking my panties off.

"What do you want, Rem?" he asked, slipping a finger inside of me.

"I want to forget."

He shook his head. "No."

I squirmed, pushing against his finger and settling a heel on his shoulder. "Just for a little while," I begged.

"That's not what our bed's for, baby."

"Merrick," I rasped.

He slid his finger out of me and I whimpered with need. He leaned over me and met my eyes. "Our bed's for makin' love and sleepin'. You wanna forget anything, you forget some other way, but if you want to heal, I'll fuck you so hard, you'll always remember who loves you. Got it?"

I swallowed, nodding and crying out when his finger slipped back inside of me, sweeping against my walls before his thumb connected with my clit.

"Look at me, baby."

I lifted my head slightly and watched him smile. "You come every time you wanna come, yeah?"

I nodded.

"Don't wait."

"Okay, Tweety." I dropped my head back to the mattress and pressed into his hand.

He added a finger then another, before he moved, faster and faster, his palm slapping against my clit as his fingers fucked me hard and deep. I gripped his wrist, stilling him, lifting my hips as an orgasm washed over me, then he was kneeling between my legs and his girth was filling me and I felt home.

He kissed me, burying himself deeper and deeper, and once again, an orgasm came hard and fast. I dug my heels into his ass and let the climax wash over me as unbidden tears slid down my cheeks.

"Fuck," he whispered, shifting so he could thumb my tears gently away. "Baby, don't cry."

"I'm okay, Tweety. You just make everything so much better."

"And that's why you're crying?"

I nodded. "Yes. Don't stop, Tweety. Please. I'll die if you stop."

He pushed in further and I raised one leg higher to take him deep, so deep I felt like he was touching my womb and slid my hands into his hair. Then he kissed me, and I kissed him back, the movement of his hips making my pussy ripple in response.

"Merr," I breathed out, another orgasm building.

His hand cupped my breast, his fingers rolling my nipple to a tight bud, and I let myself go. He wasn't far behind, evidenced by the low grunt he gave me, and his hand moving to grip my thigh as he came inside of me.

He kissed me as he rolled us onto our sides, my legs still wrapped around his waist and his dick still buried deep.

"I'll marry you," I whispered.

"Yeah?"

I nodded. "I know we have a lot to figure out, but I can't imagine my life without you for a day, let alone a lifetime."

He stroked my cheek and smiled. "Same, honey."

"I like this kind of healing. It's very Marvin Gaye."

He chuckled, kissing me quickly, then sliding out of me and heading to the bathroom. I climbed under the covers just as he returned with a warm washcloth that he settled between my legs to clean me up. Chucking the cloth in the corner, he climbed in beside me and pulled me over his chest.

"I wanna take you home next week."

"I thought you were here for two," I countered.

"Yeah, baby, but I think we should do the memorial service, then head home. It's not safe here."

"What about Kennedy?"

"She's ours now, Rem. She'll be protected."

I settled my chin on my hand and met his eyes. "What do you mean she's yours?"

"Mouse has claimed her."

"What?" I sat up. "How do you know that?"

He grinned in response.

"She won't like it."

Merrick shrugged. "I highly doubt he'll give a shit."

"Honey, you have to warn him." I shook my head. "Not to speak ill of my bestie, but she's a ball-buster. Like, a serious one…it's a sport for her."

"Pretty sure he can handle it."

"He's probably ten years younger than her."

"So?"

"*So,* he's a baby." I dragged my hands down my face. "She'll eat him alive."

"And he'll love every second."

"Jebus, he's in for a challenge."

Merrick tugged me down on top of him again. "I have it on good authority he likes a challenge."

I sighed and snuggled closer again. "I guess if he likes a challenge…"

"You done worrying about everyone else?"

"Probably not," I admitted.

"It's all good, Eeyore." He grinned, kissing me again. "You wouldn't be you if you didn't worry, and I happen to love everything about you."

"Are you going to have time to help me with the bank stuff on Monday?"

"I gave you everything. Do you need me to hold your hand?"

I glanced up at him. "Kinda."

"I have some casework I need to get moving on, but we can do it after lunch."

"Am I going to be able to take a couple of classes?"

His body stiffened. "Where?"

"At Parker."

Parker Conservatory had been my home away from home ever since I'd started dancing at five years old. Whenever I could drop in for a class I would, although, my chances had been few and far between of late.

"That doesn't help me, Rem. Need to know where."

"Oh, of course."

I gave him the general vicinity, since he wouldn't know the location by the address and he seemed to relax a bit.

"You set it up and I'll take you and pick you up," he said. "Just not Monday."

"Okay." I bit back a yawn, burrowing further into him.

"You gonna sleep now?"

"Yes. Don't leave, okay?"

"I'm right here, Rem."

I closed my eyes and slept.

THIRTEEN

Remington

THURSDAY MORNING, I was bouncing off the walls, needing *out* of the compound. Monday had been a shit show with Merrick's schedule, so I was forced to call the bank instead of going inside the building, which was fine, I was able to get enough information to order checks and such. But then he got stuck on a conference call with a client on Tuesday so by the time he got off, the class I'd wanted to join was over, which totally blew my plans since he refused to let anyone else take me.

Wednesday, I'd worked on a slide show for Natalie, and going through old photos from Michelle's life with me and Kennedy had been tough. So much so, I was snappy with Merrick all day, until he finally fucked me back into some semblance of normalcy that evening.

But now it was Thursday, and he'd wandered off to

some private office somewhere in the back of the compound, and I was done.

"You look like you're about to pitch a hissy," Alamo observed, walking into the kitchen where I'd just poured my third cup of coffee. Alamo was tall, built, and had a kickass beard that begged to be touched. I didn't for obvious reasons, the least of which being Jasmine would cut me into a million pieces, and the most of which being I was in love with my own man.

"Whatever gave you that idea?" I deadpanned.

He smiled. "You need something?"

"I need out of this goddamn building."

"Finch not around?"

I shrugged. "I haven't seen him for over an hour. He's been stuck on some conference call for a year now, so I have a feeling I'm not gonna see him anytime soon."

"He not good with a recruit shuttling you?"

"Apparently not," I said with a sigh.

He checked his watch. "I got a few. Want me to take you somewhere?"

I bit my lip. "There's a class starting in twenty minutes at Parker, you know over on third?"

"The arts place?"

I nodded.

"Yeah, I can take you."

"Oh my god, that would be amazing. I'll just grab my stuff."

I made a run for Merrick's room, changing into a leotard and shoving toe shoes and sweats into a tote in record time. I met Alamo back downstairs in less than ten minutes, and we headed out to his truck.

"Did you let Finch know we're leaving?" he asked as I climbed up into his truck.

"Um, no, I'll do that now," I promised and pulled out my phone.

Alamo climbed into the cab and faced me. "All good?"

"Yep."

Technically, I hadn't heard back from Merrick, but I doubted he'd be concerned if I was with Alamo. And since I was a grown-ass adult, and I was with the Sergeant at Arms for a badass motorcycle club, I figured Merrick would be fine with it.

Little did I know I figured wrong. Very wrong.

* * *

Finch

I came up for air just before lunch and headed upstairs to look for Remington. My phone was currently charging in my room, considering I'd lost juice about an hour into my conference call with Mack. She wasn't there, so I snagged my phone off the nightstand and headed back downstairs.

As I descended the stairs, I read my texts and stalled. "What the fuck?" I snapped. I stalked downstairs and bellowed, "Alamo!"

"Yo!" he called back, and I followed the sound.

"Where the fuck's Remington?" I demanded, walking into the kitchen.

"At her dance class."

"Alone?"

"No. Stump's on her."

"Goddammit, I said no one but me."

"I'm out, man." He raised his hands in surrender. "She said you were cool. I'm supposed to be picking her up in half an hour, but you feel free to go since you seem to be free."

I nodded. This had nothing to do with Alamo and I didn't doubt that Remington had led him to believe all was cool.

Alamo jotted down the address and I grabbed the keys to my rental and headed out. I took a couple of deep breaths in an effort to calm down. The last thing I needed was to get pulled over.

Arriving at the conservatory, I saw Stump's bike out front, but refused to relax, especially since Remington and I had had a very clear and concise conversation about her movements. I walked into the building and saw Stump leaning up against a wall at the end of the hallway, so I headed that way.

"Thanks, brother. I got her," I said, and Stump nodded.

I could tell he knew something was up, but walked away without comment and I stood where he'd just been a few minutes ago.

Fuming.

* * *

Remington

I flopped down on the floor after the workout of the century, my body on fire, but my mind finally quieted, as I pulled off my toe shoes and yanked on sweats and tennies.

I still hadn't received a return text from Merrick, so I hoped he was just busy and not mad at me. Luckily, I'd have some backup in the form of Alamo should Merrick decide to get pissy.

Madame Sellers made her way to me and gave me a big smile. "You've been working hard, Remington. You looked beautiful."

"Thank you."

"We are looking for talented instructors for the fall season, in case you're interested. We'd love to have you."

"Oh, wow. Um, thank you. I'm not sure where I'll be in the fall, but I can let you know."

"I'll need to know by the beginning of next month."

"I'll keep that in mind," I promised.

I slung my bag over my shoulder and walked toward the exit, stalling when I walked out to find a very angry, however, very delicious looking Tweety. "Hey, honey."

He scowled, but said nothing.

Okay, pissy is the way it's going, apparently.

"Did you get my text?"

"Yeah," he grunted, taking my bag from me.

"But you're mad."

"Mad doesn't even touch what I am, Remington."

Shit.

"Why?"

"We'll talk back at the compound."

"Um, no, we'll talk now."

"Not having this conversation in a public place, Rem," he growled.

"You cannot be mad."

He scowled again and settled his hand on my lower back to guide me toward the doors.

"Tweety, you were busy. Alamo brought me. Not a recruit."

Pushing open the door, he held it while I walked out. "And yet, Stump was in the hall waiting on you."

"What?" I whispered. "He was?"

"Yeah, Rem. He was."

Well, crap. That was definitely against the rules. On the other hand, Alamo trusted Stump, and Alamo's a bigwig in the club, so Merrick should be fine with it.

"I didn't know."

"Don't give a fuck," he growled.

He threw my bag in the back of his rental car and opened the door for me. I climbed in and he made his way to the driver's side.

"Alamo approved Stump, right?" I asked once Merrick started the car.

"Did I?"

"No, but you were busy, so Alamo offered—"

"Alamo is *not* your man."

"What does that have to do with anything?"

"I told you I would take you out."

"On Monday, you told me you'd take me out. Then again on Tuesday, but you were busy. Now it's Thursday, and I had to take a class."

"You could have waited until I was done."

"When did you get done, Merrick? Huh?"

"Not the point."

"It *is* the point," I snapped. "You've been keeping me locked up in your fortress without access to human contact."

"Babe. There are close to fifty humans for you to have contact with," he argued. "Not close contact, over the kitchen island or through a door, but human contact, nonetheless."

"I want contact with *my* humans," I ground out. "The ones I'm allowed to hug."

"Then you wait until I can take you where you need to go."

"Or I can go stay with Kennedy."

"You're not fucking leaving the compound until we figure out who the threat is."

"You have the threat," I countered. "Seth."

"Seth's a pawn."

"But he was the one who killed those girls, right? So, the threat's been eliminated for now."

Before Merrick could counter with some stupid ass explanation, my phone rang, and I welcomed the distraction. "Hello."

"Remington Aultman Charles, what's this about you being back in town and I have not received a phone call?" my mother accused, her southern accent on ten.

"Hi, Mom."

"Don't 'hi, Mom' me, young lady. We still have Sunday dinner every week, I expect you to be there."

"Mom, Michelle's memorial service is Sunday," I said. "And then I'm leaving Tuesday."

That part was a lie. I didn't know when I was leaving…or if I actually was. Merrick raised an eyebrow and I focused forward as I tried to avoid both my mother and my boyfriend.

"Leaving? Leaving to go where?"

"Back to Portland."

"Are you still on that ridiculous road?"

"So, did you need something?" I asked, diverting the subject.

"Daddy and I would love to see you. Perhaps take you out to dinner."

"That sounds lovely," I lied. "Let me look at my calendar and send you a few dates."

"Wonderful, darlin'. We'll talk soon."

"Okay, Mom, bye."

"So, you're coming home with me, then?" Merrick asked after I hung up.

"I don't know yet," I said.

"Are you fucking kidding me?"

"Merrick—"

"When exactly are you going to have time to see your parents?"

"Oh, I'm not. They can go fuck themselves. But I can't say that to them. I play the game."

"Jesus," he hissed. "How many people do you play this game with?"

"Only them," I said.

"Wish I believed that," he grumbled as we drove through the compound gates.

"Don't be melodramatic."

"Don't fuckin' tell me I'm bein' melodramatic when my woman makes me a promise, then breaks it."

"I didn't break a promise."

"You broke a promise."

I scoffed. "I told you I had to get out. I had to take a class, or I'd go crazy. If anyone broke a promise, it was you."

Merrick let out a frustrated grunt and stomped out of the car. I knew we were at an impasse, so I climbed out and walked into the compound, not caring if he followed or not.

I passed Alamo as I stormed up the stairs, but decided I was kind of pissed at him too, so didn't acknowledge his existence as I made my way to Merrick's room. I walked inside, stripped off my clothes, and stepped into the shower.

I was still pretty riled up as I dried off and dressed, partly because Merrick hadn't come up to check on me or make sure I was okay. Irrational, granted, but I wanted him to apologize and bow before his queen in contrition.

I slid on a pair of tennies and headed downstairs to find no one but Stump in the great room. He was on his phone, but rang off when he saw me. "Hey, babe. You good?"

"Have you seen Merrick?"

He looked at me in confusion.

"Finch," I corrected.

"Yeah, he's on a call. Back office."

I bit my lip, deciding just how mad I was still, before turning on my heel and heading that way.

"Yeah, Monday," I heard Merrick say. "Tuesday'll work. Okay. See you then."

I pushed open the door and leaned against the doorjamb. He met my eyes, but didn't smile. "You feeling better?"

I shrugged. "Depends on what I'm supposed to feel better about."

"I see we're still at a stalemate." He closed a file folder and set his phone on top of it.

"Stop being a dick and we won't be."

"I'm a dick because I want you safe?" he ground out. "Okay, Rem. I'm a dick, then."

"Oh my god, Merrick, stop twisting my words."

"They're your words, baby. Can't twist them when I'm repeating them verbatim."

"I have never once said I thought you were a dick for wanting me safe," I countered.

He sighed. "I want this to be a teachable moment for you, Remington."

"Excuse me?"

"You need to listen—"

"Fuck you, Merrick. You're not my father, and I'm not a child. You don't get to talk to me like that," I snapped, and stormed away.

Stump was exactly where I left him, and I closed the distance between us. "I need to run an errand."

"Let me know what you need, and I'll do it for you."

"I need to do it."

"No can do, babe. You're locked down."

"Excuse me?"

"You're locked down," Merrick repeated as he walked into the room.

I turned on him. "Meaning what, exactly?"

"Meaning, unless I say otherwise, you don't leave the compound."

"You can't do that."

"I can, baby, and I did."

"What about class or the memorial service?"

"Class is out for the moment, but I'll take you to the service. I've cleared Sunday."

"Oh, how generous of you, benevolent one," I spat out. "Please put some time on your calendar to kindly fuck yourself as well."

With that, I headed back upstairs where I locked myself into the room and flopped onto the bed. I was so mad, I couldn't even cry.

But I could scheme. And I did. In the form of Merrick's murder and all the ways I could hide his body.

FOURTEEN

Finch

R EMINGTON WAS STILL distant with me as I took her hand toward the end of Michelle's memorial service. We'd made a tentative truce on Friday after she'd given me the silent treatment for over twenty-four hours, but I could still feel her shutting down and I hated it.

She let me take her hand but pulled away when the pastor ended the service and she hugged Michelle's family. Even though I offered my hand again, she didn't take it as we walked out of the little chapel Michelle had been dedicated in when she was a baby. The whole thing was sad as fuck and I was surprised Remington didn't completely break down on me. I figured that would probably come later.

"I'm going to the bathroom," she said to no one in particular, so I moved to follow.

"Do you need to watch me pee, Merrick, or am I allowed to do that on my own?" she snarled.

I sighed. "I'll wait for you here."

"Thank you, gracious and benevolent one."

I rolled my eyes. Apparently, the truce was over.

"Hey." I took her hand pulled her against me. "I love you."

She stared over me. "Hmm-mm."

I kissed her gently, but she didn't kiss me back, so I watched her walk through the ladies' door then pulled out my phone to check messages. I had to meet with a client on Tuesday, which meant a long day of travel tomorrow to get back to Portland in time, but at least, Remington would be with me and I'd know she was safe.

"Where's Remi?" Kennedy asked.

I lifted my chin toward the bathroom.

Kennedy nodded and walked inside, stepping out again within seconds. "Finch, she's not in there."

"Come again?"

"The bathroom's empty. No Remington."

I shoved past her and pushed into the bathroom, checking every stall, and Kennedy was right. She'd disappeared. I saw a window at the back of the room was open, and my blood ran cold. "Fuck," I snapped, and grabbed my phone, texting Alamo.

"She's probably back inside," Kennedy said. "You just didn't see her leave the bathroom."

"I would have seen her, Kennedy."

"Let me go look."

Mouse was heading our way and I gave him a chin lift. "You stay here, babe."

"What's up?" Mouse asked.

"Remington's missing, lock Kennedy down. Eyes on her at all times."

"No problem," Mouse said, although Kennedy wasn't too happy with my edict.

I didn't give a fuck as I headed outside and tried to figure out where the hell she was, calling Booker on the way.

"Hey, Finch."

"Need you to track Remington's phone."

"Shit, she okay?"

I filled him in on what I knew, hanging up just as the sound of pipes roared around me. Alamo, along with three other Dogs, rode into the parking lot and I walked toward them.

"What do we know?" Alamo asked.

"Rem was in the bathroom, then she wasn't. I think she got out through the window at the back, but there's no sign of her." I dragged my hands through my hair. "I have no idea if she left on her own or someone took her. Booker's tracking her phone."

"Okay. Get Kennedy to give you a list of where she might go to be alone. We'll start—"

"Finch!" Kennedy called, rushing toward me, Mouse hot on her heels. "Remington dropped her grandma's ring." She handed it to me. "She would never let that out of her sight. She always used to joke that the only way anyone would get it was off her cold, dead body."

I hissed out a breath and Kennedy shook her head. "Not that I think she's dead. Far from it. She would have dropped it to let you know she didn't go of her own free will."

I stroked the platinum band with a nod, then slid it onto my pinky finger. It would stay there until I found her.

* * *

Remington

My head felt like a vice grip was squeezing it and my mouth was as dry as wallpaper…I figured out pretty quickly it was dry because I had a gag over it. I also discovered my hands and feet were tied…tight. I glanced down my body and bit back tears. Cable ties. Not easy to work your way out of.

I forced a deep breath through my nose, trying not to panic. I was horribly claustrophobic and suffocating to death was my biggest fear, so a gag in the mouth was not conducive to me not panicking. I looked around the room, trying to determine where I was, but it was dark, other than a little light coming through a transom window above me. I was on a mattress with no bedding, and I was freezing.

The sound of a door slamming and footsteps on wooden stairs had me closing my eyes and trying to relax my body enough to pretend like I was still out.

A feminine voice was whispering in Russian, but I could only make out a couple of words…they weren't nice, which indicated to me this person wasn't happy.

"No one saw me, *brat*," she snapped, switching to English.

Brother. She was speaking to her brother.

"The medicine will take a little while to wear off. You have time to get here."

Shit. Get where?

"No, she's out cold. *Da*. So easy. Okay."

The woman shuffled closer to me and I felt her breath on my cheek. "I don't understand what is so special about you," she whispered. "But I suppose we'll soon find out, won't we?"

I forced myself not to react, and it was hard when she touched my face, but I kept my breathing even and when I heard her footsteps move away from me, I waited a few minutes before opening my eyes again.

Rubbing my face against the mattress, I managed to slide the fabric tied around my mouth down, letting it settle around my neck. I took a couple of deep breaths, reminding myself I was still alive. I maneuvered my body in a way to slide my feet behind me and through my arms, tugging at the bindings around my wrists. Thank the lord for ballet, because I could pretty much contort any part of myself in any direction, so I was now able to sit up with my hands in front of me. The plastic was too tight to worm my way out of, so unless there was a knife somewhere around, I wouldn't be able to break the hold.

The dress I was wearing had pockets, but my phone had been removed, leaving me with a Chapstick and tissues. My purse was also nowhere near me. I wish I hadn't given Merrick the cold shoulder. He'd tried to apologize, and I'd still given him monosyllabic conversation. God damn my ability to hold a grudge. It got me nowhere and I still held onto my anger. Merrick was going to think I ran away again and that was on me.

Shit! I was on my own here. I mean, what were the odds they'd find my grandmother's ring? I *did* have a modicum of hope that Merrick would at least look for me, but he was in an unfamiliar city, so his chances of finding me quickly were slim.

Plus, I had to pee.

I heard the door again, so I pulled my gag back up and contorted my body back the way it was, laying back down on the mattress. Unfortunately, the bedframe squeaked, so I couldn't continue to feign being unconscious.

"You are awake," a deep voice observed, and I froze. "Good."

Vitaly.

* * *

Finch

Savannah didn't have many bad spots, but the place we were currently hauling ass toward certainly qualified as one of them, if not the worst. Alamo, Doom, Badger, and Dash rode tight behind me as we sped our way to the south side's industrial district, a mostly derelict part of town that had been abandoned after the industrial crash of the late seventies. I took Doc's Fatboy directly from the memorial, needing the comfort and speed of a bike, rather than the cage of my rental.

I kept my thoughts focused on the road ahead, rather than allowing myself to think about what that animal could be doing to Remington, or what I'd do to him when I found him. *If* I found him. Fuck that. I had to find him; the alternative meant losing Remington, and that was not going to happen.

I signaled to the others and we turned right into a small housing development that looked like it had seen better days. We passed through darkening streets lined with dilapidated houses with boarded up windows and overgrown lawns until we arrived at the address Booker had given me. I'd reached out to my VP to track her again, and he'd had trouble, considering her phone was off. But he was able to trace the phone up until the signal died, and this was where it led us.

We killed our engines, parked our bikes around the corner, and made the rest of the way on foot.

"What the hell is this place?" I asked as we reached the only two-story house on a street of otherwise modest single story, ranch style homes.

"This development was built for the employees of Kimble and Graham, back when they used to have a big factory here," Alamo explained. "The plan was to keep the employees close to where they worked to increase productivity. This house belonged to the factory foreman. When the plant closed in the early eighties, the neighborhood became a ghost town. All the families were relocated when the company moved out west, and all of these houses have been empty ever since. About ten years ago the meth heads moved in."

"Remind me to call HGTV when we get back. I've got a show to pitch them," Badger said.

"Well, according to Booker, this is where they've got

her," I said as we arrived at the house. My phone buzzed so I pulled it out and glanced at the screen. It was a text from Hatch. "Fuck."

"What?" Alamo asked.

"Vitaly. He's not in Russia. He's here."

"How do you want to play this?" Alamo asked.

"We can't see shit from here," I said. "Let's go."

"Hold on."

"No. Vitaly's got her," I argued.

"We don't have any idea at all what we're walking into here. We don't even know if it *is* Vitaly or how many people are in that house," Doom said.

"Or if she's even in there. Could just be meth heads like Alamo said," Badger said.

"Booker's intel is always solid, as you well know. If he said she's here, she's here," Alamo said.

Or she *was* here when someone turned off her phone. I could only hope she hadn't been moved since.

"Then what the fuck are we waiting for? I'm gonna move in closer to get a better look," I said, and started walking toward to the house.

"Finch, goddammit! Get back here!" Alamo whisper shouted, but I ignored him.

I crept through the high grass to the east side of the house and crouched beneath a window that had been replaced with faded plywood. I stayed very still and listened but heard nothing.

Goddammit. I should have followed her into the fucking bathroom.

I'd never been more worried or scared in my entire life, yet I still managed to be angry over the fact that by icing me out, she'd allowed herself to be placed in this situation. Why did she always have to be so damned headstrong; so difficult? Why couldn't she just fucking trust me?

Of course, I knew the answers, but having her push me away still hurt. More so now that I was in danger of losing her. I already knew that I loved her, but now I knew that I truly *needed* her.

She was difficult. She was stubborn, moody, and dramatic as hell, and I loved her. In truth, she was the most perfect woman in the world, and she was the love of my life, but she was also in grave danger. At that moment, I knew two things for sure. I couldn't stand to lose Remington, and if I didn't find her right now, she was going to die.

"Fuck this," I whispered to myself and stood up. I motioned for the others to spread out and made my way to the front entrance.

Alamo quickened his pace when he saw me going for the door and began waving his arms wildly. I paused and allowed him to catch up.

"What the fuck are you doing?" he whispered.

"I'm not waiting any longer," I said. "If you want to stop me, you're gonna have to shoot me."

Alamo pulled out a .9mm and raised it. My body locked briefly, but then he handed it to me and nodded.

"I'm right behind you," he said, before producing a revolver from his rear waistband.

I quietly tried the front doorknob and found it was unlocked. Slowly pushing the door open to a dark and quiet home, Dash, Doom, and Badger joined us as we made our way inside. Doom headed upstairs, Dash and Badger followed, and Alamo and I split up to do a sweep of the first floor.

The kitchen, dining room, and den all appeared to be as empty as the entryway. In fact, there were little to no signs of recent activity anywhere in the house.

"Didn't you say this neighborhood is filled with squatters and druggies?" I asked Alamo as we continued to sweep the spacious downstairs.

"Yeah, why?"

"Isn't this place a little clean?"

"Looks like a shithole to me," he replied.

"Sure, but if you were a homeless junkie wouldn't you want to crash at the nicest pad on the block?"

"I guess so, sure."

"Then, where the fuck is everyone? Why aren't there scumbags everywhere? This place is too clean and too quiet for a neighborhood like this."

Dash and Badger came downstairs to join us.

"The second floor's all clear," Dash said. "Doom's checkin' the attic."

"I hate to say it, but it looks like no one's here," Alamo said.

My heart raced. Where the hell was Remi? Did they somehow know we were coming and move her? Was she ever even here? My pulse raced, and my head began to throb. A dull echo pounded in my skull as my thoughts went to Remington in the hands of Vitaly. What choice did I have now? All I could do was think. I sure as hell couldn't act on any kind of a plan. I had no idea where she was. I couldn't be more helpless. I couldn't get any lower.

Lower.

"There's a basement."

"What?" Alamo asked.

"There's a lower floor," I said. "This is definitely Vitaly's place."

"What? I don't get it."

"That's why the place is so clean. Vitaly probably pays the junkies to stay clear of the place, and he keeps the house empty, so no one knows what he's up to."

I quickly went back to the hallway and began to look for any kind of basement entrance but found nothing. "It's gotta be here somewhere," I said.

"Look, man, maybe we just have the wrong place," Dash said.

I ignored him and went back to the kitchen and noticed that the walk-in pantry door was wide open.

"Did you open that door?" I asked Alamo, who shook

his head.

I raised my gun and made my way to the pantry, the others behind me. Sure enough, on the pantry floor was a trap door with a silver handle and an electronic security keypad.

"Shit," I breathed out.

FIFTEEN

Remington

VITALY LIMPED TOWARD me and I grimaced at the sight of his ugly face. "What do you want?"

He was supposed to be in Russia. I had no idea how he even got here, or how far he'd go to make me pay. I'd been scared before, but now I was terrified.

"What you didn't give me before," he spat out.

I scowled. "You'll get nothing from me, you piece of shit."

He ran his hand up my leg. "I'll get what I came for, Remington, and you'll like it."

Using the strength of my core, I raised my legs and kicked him as hard as I could. It barely made a dent, but it did get him off-kilter, which meant I could sit up and get my hands in front of me again.

It made no difference. He dragged me up, threw me onto a table, akin to a massage table and tied me down, before he proceeded to hit me in various parts of my body until I nearly passed out.

But when his sister bent down to snarl at me, I was so disgusted that this cow was defying the girl-code, I waited until she was close and bit her cheek as hard as I could. Something cracked the back of my head, then everything went black.

* * *

Finch

"You were right," Alamo said.

"Yeah, but there's a keypad on the door. How the hell are we supposed to get in without the combination?" Dash asked.

Alamo ran a hand though his hair. "He's right. It could be anything."

"Maybe we can blast the lock," Badger said.

"If he hears us coming, he'll kill her for sure," I said. My mind raced, barely able to focus. I was going insane with the thought of being so close to her but still unable to reach her. To protect her from Vitaly. That smug Russian prick would pay if he hurt her. Suddenly, I was hit with a bolt of pure clarity and blurted out, "1776."

"What?" Alamo asked.

"The code! Try 1776."

Alamo did as I instructed, and the pin pad flashed green. Not only was it the year of America's independence, it was also the year the Bolshoi Ballet was founded. Considering the fact Vitaly was extremely proud of his lineage, I took a guess.

Of course, the only reason I knew any of this was because I'd had to grill Grace on all things ballet when she was studying for her entrance exam into PBC. It was a longshot, but it was one that paid off.

"What the fuck?" he asked in total amazement.

"I'll explain later, let's get down there."

I led the way to the bottom of the staircase, my Maglite providing our only light. At the bottom of the stairs was a large room with floor to ceiling shelves lining all four walls. On those shelves where gallon jugs of water, canned goods, and non-perishable food stacked high and deep. At the end of the giant doomsday pantry was a doorway that led to long, left and right hallways, illuminated by LED baseboard lights. The basement was sleek, looked newly constructed, and was nothing like the rest of the house. It also looked like someone had spent considerable time and money on this secret underground lair. Soundproofing included.

At the end of each hallway was a single, very serious looking door. We split up, with me and Badger taking the door on the left, leaving Alamo and Dash to check the on the right. No sooner had they began walking when the door opened quickly with a whoosh and a distracted young, raven-haired woman appeared holding a wad of gauze to her face.

"I can't believe that little bitch bit me," she muttered to herself as she marched, head down, straight into Alamo's chest. She let out a high-pitched scream, dropping the gauze to reveal a bloody right cheek.

"Hey there," Alamo said, sounding unsure. None of us knew if we were encountering another one of Vitaly's victims, or something else. However, before Alamo could react, she cleared things up by producing a three-inch blade and sticking Alamo deep in the abdomen.

Before he fell to his knees, Alamo cracked his assailant directly in the forehead with the butt of his gun, and she dropped like a stone onto the carpeted hallway floor.

"Aw, shit man, I've never hit a woman before," Alamo said, falling to his side, blood pouring from his gut.

"Call 9-1-1!" I shouted to Dash, who immediately

reached for his phone.

"Alamo!" Badger yelled as he began to apply pressure to the wound.

"Tell her I'm sorry I hit her okay?" Alamo said, his color greying.

"Jesus, man, he's bad!" Badger cried out as door number two swung open.

I couldn't see anyone standing in the doorway, but this door opened in the same whooshing fashion as the other, leading me to believe they were activated hydraulically.

"Nadia! What the fuck is going on out there?" I heard Vitaly call out.

I turned to the others, held my index finger to my lips, and took two silent steps toward the door before he called out again.

"Nadia, you spoiled brat. You'd better not be throwing one of your tantrums or breaking anything out there! She barely even nipped you. Besides…" he said, his voice getting louder. "…I made sure Remington paid for what she did to your pretty face."

He looked up from cleaning his hands with a bloody rag as he said this, and our eyes connected. I raised my gun and he dropped his grin. I didn't hesitate to squeeze the trigger and put two holes directly into his chest.

"Remington!" I cried out as I ran to the doorway. Vitaly was still alive and conscious when I reached him, but appeared unable to move, so I stepped over him and ran into the room to find Remington.

"Frisk him," I heard someone say behind me.

Knowing they'd make sure Vitaly was taken care of, I focused on finding Remington. I almost passed out when I saw her. She was strapped to a table. Her ankles and right arm were bound, and she had been beat to a pulp. Her left arm was free but was clearly broken, hanging down like a mangled bird's wing.

Fearing the worst, I watched her chest until I saw the

labored rise and fall that assured me she was still breathing. Determined to keep her that way, I rushed in and took in the damage.

"Oh, my God baby, what did he do to you?" Tears streamed down my face as I gently kissed Remington's bloodied face. A face that at that moment barely resembled her. Her eyes were closed, lips parted, the left side of her face was already darkening with a giant bruise, and a gash ran along her cheek, leaking blood. "Remi, babe, I need you to wake up."

She didn't respond.

There was so much fucking blood, I didn't know where to start or whether or not I should move her. What if something was broken?

"The ambulance is coming baby. Just hold on okay?" I said as I removed her restraints. At least I could do that. I heard Vitaly's moans from the doorway and whispered to Remington, "I'll be right back, I promise."

I couldn't do shit about Remington, but I sure as fuck could do something about the asshole who'd done this to her. I walked to Vitaly and bent down, so he could see my face clearly.

"Please… help me," he sputtered as blood poured from his mouth.

"I'm not here to help you, you son-of-a-bitch. I want you looking into my eyes when I send you to hell."

I squeezed the trigger again. Point blank. Right through the motherfucker's heart. As the echo of the .9mm rang out through the hallway, I could hear the sirens of the approaching ambulance.

"Give me that," Dash demanded, and took the gun from me. I dropped to my knees and felt Vitaly for a weapon.

"This was on him," Dash said, passing me a knife.

I grabbed the bandana I had in my pocket, wiped the knife down, pressed Vitaly's fingerprints all over it, and placed it on the ground next to him, curling his fingers around the hilt.

"Was he left or right-handed?" I asked to no one in particular.

"You need to get the fuck outta here," Badger pressed, still holding pressure on Alamo's wound.

"I am *not* leaving Remington," I said and took the gun back from Badger.

"I don't know who's comin', Finch. I don't know if they're friendlies."

"It's fucking self-defense, Badger." I rose to my feet. "It's all good."

"Doc's not gonna like that you shot this asshole. We don't do that."

"We do when one of ours is being threatened, brother, and you well know it. Pretty sure if Quin was in the same position, you wouldn't hesitate. Did you see what the fuck he did to Remi? Go look and tell me you wouldn't have done the same thing."

"Jesus, you've got balls of steel."

I shrugged and headed back to Remington to wait for the emergency vehicles.

"Goddammit!" a voice I didn't recognize echoed through the house.

"We got another one!" Doom called out.

I made my way toward the noise in case my brothers needed backup, and found a man I didn't recognize, gun drawn, F.B.I. written across his Kevlar vest.

"What the fuck did you do, Doom?" he growled out.

"Got somethin' for ya, Dalton." Doom shoved an older looking man to the ground and settled his foot in his back. His hands were ziptied behind him, so he was immobile for the moment. "He was hidin' in the attic. Meet Yegor Sokolov. Vitaly's uncle, and brother to one Captain Vasili Sokolov of the Iolanta. Remember him?"

"Poppy's captor," Dash provided.

"One and the same," Doom said.

"Number six on the F.B.I.'s most wanted list," Dalton said.

"You're welcome." Doom nodded. "I'm assuming you can take control of this scene?"

"Yeah, man, I'll take it from here."

* * *

Remington

I forced gritty eyes open and quickly decided I was totally over waking up in dark rooms. Pain shot through my arm and I cried out, trying to shift away from the discomfort.

"Baby?"

"Merrick?" I whispered, searching for him in the darkness.

"I'm here, honey," he said, leaning over me. "Gonna get you something for the pain."

"Where am I?"

"Hospital."

"Where's Vitaly?"

"Dead."

I gasped. "What?"

"Let me get a nurse. I'll explain everything as soon as you're feeling better."

I reached for him. "Wait."

He leaned over me again. "What, honey?"

"I'm so sorry."

"You have nothing to be sorry about." He stroked my cheek and kissed me gently. "Let me get you some pain meds."

I nodded, and he left me, but only for a minute, returning with a pretty red-headed nurse who was admiring my man a little too much for my liking.

"You're awake," she said, leaning over me with a smile.

"Thanks, Captain Obvious," I grumbled, and she

chuckled.

"Good to see you have a sense of humor." She shot something into my IV and I instantly felt relief.

I also felt happy and high.

"Better?" she asked.

I giggled in response.

She patted my arm and nodded. "I'm going to get the doctor. I'll be back in a minute."

Merrick sat on the edge of the bed and smiled. "You feeling good?"

I nodded. "My mouth is dry, though."

"I'll get you some water."

He helped me with the straw and I drank deeply. Water had never tasted so good.

A doctor walked in a few minutes later and pulled up my X-rays. "You have a pretty clean break, considering. A cast will suffice, no surgery. You have some contusions on your face as well, but nothing is broken, and I don't see evidence of a concussion, despite the beating. We'll keep you overnight, get you sorted with a cast, and you should be able to go home before lunch."

"Did you test me for rabies?" I asked.

"Were you bit by a rabid animal?" the doctor asked, concerned.

"No, I bit the bitch who was helping her brother beat the shit out of me. Just want to make sure she's clean."

The doctor relaxed. "We ran bloodwork for several possible infections. All are clean."

"Thank you," I said.

"You've got a call button right next to you, and if you have any questions, let the nurses know, okay?"

I nodded. "I will. Thank you."

The doctor left, and Merrick was by my side again. "You still feeling good?"

I nodded. "How bad does my face look?"

"Don't wanna talk about that right now," Merrick said.

"It's that bad?"

"Baby, you're beautiful. Nothing will ever change that, but it means I have to explain how many hits that asshole got in before I found you, and I don't really want to go there."

"Who killed him?"

"I did."

I burst into tears and he stretched out on the bed and pulled me against him. "You crying because he's dead or because I shot him?"

"I'm crying because you saved me and made it so he can't hurt anyone else."

"Are you okay with that?"

"Yes," I hissed. "I love you. I was a twatwaffle to you and you still saved me."

His body shook, and I knew he was laughing.

"Don't laugh at me. I'm injured."

"Twatwaffle?"

"Scientific term for bitch."

"Baby, we both had culpability in the argument. We've apologized, it's done. Now it's time to get you home and we'll figure everything else out once you're feeling better."

"You still want me to come home with you?" I whispered.

"Jesus, Rem, did you think I'd change my mind over some dumbass argument?"

"Yes, kind of."

He kissed me gently. "I love you. Nothing's gonna change that."

"Promise?"

"Yeah, honey, I promise."

"Can we get a new sofa?" I asked.

"You don't like my sofa?"

"No. It's leather. I hate leather."

"Why do you hate leather?"

"Because it's all squeaky and shit," I said. "I want to lie

down on a couch without *hearing* it."

"Okay, honey, we can get a new sofa."

"Thanks, Tweety."

"You're welcome Eeyore."

His phone buzzed and he checked his screen and swore.

"What's wrong?"

"The rabid bitch stabbed Alamo in the stomach. It's touch and go. They think she nicked his liver."

"Oh my god, Merrick. Is Jasmine okay? You should make sure."

"Don't know, honey. But she's surrounded by family, so gonna let them take care of her. You are *my* priority."

With him holding me, I fell asleep and didn't wake up again until the next morning when it was time to be fitted with a cast.

* * *

Jasmine

"Where is he?" I demanded, rushing into the emergency area of the hospital.

"They just wheeled him up for surgery," Badger said, pulling me in for a hug.

I pushed him away. "What happened? All of it, Knox McKellar. Don't filter."

"Gonna fuckin' filter a little bit, Jazz," he warned, and filled me in.

"The bitch is here too? The one who stabbed him?"

Badger nodded.

"What's her name?"

"Nadia Popov," he said.

I nodded and headed to the elevator.

"Jazz, where the fuck are you going?" Badger demanded, jogging to catch up to me.

"I'm not telling you, unless you'll agree to be my lookout."

"Fuck me, Jasmine. No."

"Then, kindly walk away, Badger."

"Jazz."

The elevator doors opened, and I stepped inside.

"Alamo's gonna fuckin' kill me," he complained as he walked into the elevator with me.

I smiled without mirth as I tried to keep my composure. I needed the muscle memory of my southern upbringing to lead me where I needed to go.

Arriving at reception, I stepped to the desk and smiled.

"May I help you?"

"Yes," I breathed out softly, hoping for a worried tone. "My friend was brought in and I'm worried sick. Would you please tell me which room Nadia Popov is in?"

"Let me look."

Badger hung back, which I was glad for, since he was wearing his badass biker gear and looking scary as hell, even if he was adorable.

"She's under guard, ma'am."

"Oh, my word," I said, placing my hand on my chest. "Is she in danger?"

"I can't say. I'm sorry."

"Is there a waiting area on her floor? I just want to know if she's okay."

"Ma'am, I am bound by the rules of this hospital."

I crossed my heart. "I promise I won't bother anyone."

She sighed. "There's a common waiting room on the fourth floor."

I gave her prayer hands. "Thank you so much."

Turning on my heel, I headed back to the elevator and pressed the button for the fourth floor.

"What's your play here, Jazz?" Badger asked.

"You're gonna find her room for me and figure out how to get me in."

"Fuck me," Badger rasped.

"Not my type, buddy, but thanks for the offer."

The doors dinged open and Badger pulled me aside gently as we stepped out. "Need you to think about this, babe. It's not a good idea."

"You have no idea if it's a good idea or not."

"You goin' after this bitch while she's in a hospital bed isn't a good idea."

I shrugged. "Who said I was going after her?"

"Jazz."

"If you're not going to help me, go ahead and leave, buddy. I'm good."

"I'm not fuckin' leavin' you, Jasmine, and you know it. Alamo'd have my fuckin' head if I did."

I raised an eyebrow. "Then, help me."

He shook his head as he sighed. "Follow me."

I grinned in triumph and followed him.

Badger pointed to a chair in the hallway and whispered, "Sit there for a sec."

I sat and pulled out my phone, so it looked like I was doing something useful. At least forty-thousand minutes went by and still no Badger. Security and real police officers roamed the floor, one of them even winked at me as he walked past, and I dropped my head again in an effort not to make eye-contact with anyone.

Jesus, where was he?

I saw him just as I was about to abort the plan and he handed me a slip of paper, but kept walking.

412.

I had no idea where he was going, but I didn't ponder it as I made my way toward room 412.

"Officer Hernandez, there's a phone call for you," I heard as I approached the room.

A uniformed police officer walked away from the door and I knew I'd hit pay dirt. I sped up my steps and slipped into the room, making sure no one else was inside, then made my way to the bed. Nadia Popov was reclined on the mattress, handcuffed to the rail, so I leaned over her. "Hello, Nadia."

Her eyes flew open. "Who are you?" she rasped.

"I'm the woman whose man you cut." I sneered down at her and wrapped my hand around her throat. I had no intention of killing her, but I was a little taken aback by how much I liked knowing I could. "I would call you a cunt, but since there's nothing warm nor deep about you, we'll just go with bitch. I'm going to make sure you go to prison for a very long time. Maybe there you'll learn how to keep the woman code and work out some of your depraved ideas of what men should be allowed to do to them. I hope you rot in hell right alongside your brother."

With that, I walked out as fast as I could just as Nadia screamed bloody murder. My heart raced as Badger reached out from a hallway and pulled me to him. "Time to go."

I stayed close to him as we tried not to run to the elevators and stepped inside. Once on the surgery waiting room floor, we headed to our family and I took deep, gulping breaths as we sat down.

"I forgot she could still use her voice," I whispered.

"Yeah, but don't worry about it," Badger said. "The cameras were disabled and won't be back up for another"— he glanced at his watch "—ten seconds."

"How…never mind, I don't want to know," I said.

He nodded and sat down beside me as we waited for information on Alamo.

SIXTEEN

Remington

WE WERE HOME.

It had been a week since we'd left Savannah, and I was healing faster than expected. I wouldn't be able to take my cast off for at least another month, but my face didn't look as though it had gone ten rounds with Ronda Rousey anymore. Alamo was healing perfectly. His liver was fine, and he was giving Jasmine a hell of a time since he didn't want to stay in bed. This was a good sign, considering how scary the whole thing had been.

Merrick had given me carte blanche to decorate his place, as long as pink didn't enter the equation. Luckily, I hated pink, but I loved paisley, so he was going to have to deal with a lot of cream and blue paisley.

He'd promised to take me shopping for a new sofa tomorrow, but tonight, he was at church, so I was home alone.

Well, until Grace showed up.

"Holy shit," she said as she hugged me, leaning back to study my face. "He really got you."

I nodded, closing the door behind her. "Yeah."

"You need to fill me in on everything." She walked to the kitchen and grabbed a bottle of wine. "Mind if I drink?"

"Go for it."

"Can you yet?"

I shook my head. "I'm still on Vicodin."

"Okay, I'll drink for you."

"Flea drove you, I take it?"

She grinned. "He sure did. Because I told him I planned to get drunk."

"I love it."

"Oh, before I get alcohol amnesia, Cassidy wants to see you dance."

I flopped onto the sofa, grimacing at the leather squeak. "She's seen me dance."

"I know, but now she wants to audition you for her new company."

"Really?" I asked.

"Yes. When she found out you were coming back, she asked me to set it up."

"Oh my god, that's amazing."

"Amazing enough not to fucking run away again?" Grace challenged.

"So, we're doin' that, huh?"

"You're damn right we're doin' that. I'm ready for your apology now, and an explanation, you can choose in which order those happen."

"Technically, I already apologized."

"But I wasn't ready to accept then. I'm ready now."

I sighed. "I'm really sorry, Grace. I shouldn't have run away like that. My feelings for your brother just totally freaked me out and I couldn't deal."

"Well, next time you can't deal, you still need to call your girl. Hos before bros."

"Okay, honey, I can do that."

"Thank you. Now fill me in on Savannah."

"It was awful," I said. "Vitaly tried to finish what he started and roped his sister into it."

"He has a sister?

I nodded. "Nadia. Total bitch."

"Sounds like it."

I filled her in on everything I remembered, pausing when I heard the locks in the door turn. It was close to eleven and Grace and I watched as our men walked in, laughing at something, then stalling when they caught sight of us.

"You okay?" Merrick asked.

"We're great," I said.

"Yeah," Grace agreed. "Why?"

"Because, darling sister, you look guilty as hell."

She giggled. "I'm tipsy, so, sure, guilty's probably accurate."

Flea grinned, walking to her and leaning down to kiss her. "You drink water in between?"

"Yes."

"You ready to go home?"

She grinned. "Yep."

He pulled her up off the sofa, and after we said goodbye, Flea took Grace home. Merrick grabbed a beer and flopped down beside me, and I settled my legs over his lap. "How was church?"

"Uneventful."

"That's good, right?"

"Yeah, baby, that's good." He set his beer down and took one of my feet in his hands. "How are you feeling?"

"My arm's being a little bitch today. I had to take a pain pill about an hour ago."

"You need anything?"

I wiggled my foot in his hand. "Less talky, more rubby would be appreciated."

He chuckled squeezing my foot. "Okay, baby."

"Grace said Cassidy wants to audition me."

"Yeah?"

I nodded. "Should I do it?"

"Do you want to?"

"Kinda, yeah."

"Then, do it."

"Okay."

He studied me. "You feeling weird about it?"

"Merrick, I'm not a size zero. I have to bind my boobs every time I perform, I've tried to shrink my butt, but nothing ever seems to work."

"You're fucking beautiful, Rem."

I took a deep breath. "I'm not saying I'm not beautiful, honey. Will you listen, *please*?"

He raised his hands in surrender and nodded.

"Outside of the fact I've eaten like a woman twice my size these last couple of weeks, I am not the 'ideal' ballerina size. I know that. I accept that. I cut weight when I have to, but unless I want a breast reduction, there's nothing I can do about the girls. I'm a hard sell. I have always known it, so I try to work three times as hard as other girls because I know I have stuff to overcome they don't. It's fine, honestly, I'm not being a sad-sack about it."

"Then, what?"

"I'm just feeling a little insecure, I guess." I sighed. "I just don't want her to feel obligated to audition me because I'm yours."

"You must not know the same Cassidy as I do."

"You think?"

"I *know*." He shifted, settling one of my legs to his right and the other to his left so he could kneel between them, sliding his head under my T-shirt and kissing my belly, careful to avoid the bruises.

I giggled as I squirmed under his touch. "What are you doing?"

"Whatever do you mean?" he said in a sing-song voice. "I'm investigating."

"Investigating what?"

"What my woman could possibly have to feel insecure about."

"Cassidy's amazing, Tweety. As is Grace. I can't compare to them."

He pushed my T-shirt further up, then tugged one cup of my bra down, exposing my nipple. "Did they say they wanted you to compare?" he challenged, drawing a nipple into his mouth, then blowing on it, the cold making it pebble into a tight peak.

"No." I slid my hands into his hair, arching into his touch. "But they want someone at their level and I'm not sure I am."

"That's a lie," he said, unclasping my bra at the front and freeing both my breasts.

"You haven't seen me—"

"Dance," he interrupted, moving to the waistband of my yoga pants. "Yes, I have. Lift."

I lifted, and he tugged them down my hips and off, panties and all. "You've seen a few minutes of a class, that's not the same."

"You forget that I've been ensconced in the ballet world for longer than I'd like, which means, I've picked up a shit ton of knowledge about who's good and who's not. I even had to quiz Grace when she was studying for the written portion of her entrance exam in PBC." He slid down my body, spreading my knees and running his finger between my already slick folds. "You are *good*, Rem. Better than good." His mouth landed on my mound, and I arched into him, my good hand instinctively weaving into his hair.

He licked and sucked me into a frenzy, then he stood and removed his clothes in record time, settling between my legs again and sliding into me. As he began to move, the squeak from the leather gave me uncontrollable giggles, so we were forced to vacate the living room.

"New sofa tomorrow," he growled as we rushed to the bedroom. "Lean over the bed, tits to the mattress."

I did as instructed, and Merrick slid his hand between my legs.

"Wider, Rem."

I spread wider and was rewarded with a slap on my ass. I squirmed, the need for him inside of me great. "Merrick," I begged.

"What do you want, baby?"

"I want you to fuck me."

His hand cupped my mound and he gave my pussy a gentle smack.

"You gonna show me how flexible you are?"

"God, yes," I hissed as his fingers slid inside of me.

He pulled his fingers out and slapped my pussy again. "Then, *spread*, Rem."

I spread into a split and he stopped me where he wanted me, which was almost to the floor. He knelt behind me and his hand went back between my legs, his fingers dragging my wetness from front to back. "You good?"

"Yes," I whispered, my pussy convulsing as he slid his fingers inside of me, while his thumb pressed against my asshole. "More, baby."

He kissed me between my shoulder blades and slid his fingers further in. He slid his other hand around me, fingering my clit as he kept me anchored, his chest to my back. "More?"

I shook my head, crying out as I came, every part of my body shaking with climax.

"Fuck," he breathed out. "Are you okay?"

"Yes," I said, dropping my head to his shoulder and gulping in deep breaths. "More now."

"Yeah?"

"Yeah," I panted out. "I want your dick inside of me. Everywhere."

"Let's put a pin in that, I don't have lube."

I wrinkled my nose. "Then why'd your fingers just write a check your dick couldn't cash?"

"I kinda went with it. Didn't know you'd be up for it."

"Newsflash Tweety, I'm up for it," I ground out. "New sofa *and* lube tomorrow."

He chuckled. "Okay, baby. We'll make it a priority."

He lifted me onto the bed and leaned over me. I slid a leg up to his shoulder, wrapping the other around his waist. "I'll settle for your dick in my pussy, Tweety, but you better make it worth my while."

His hand cupped my breast and he grinned. "I'm in service to the queen."

He slammed into me and I mewed as his dick hit my G-spot.

"Don't come yet, baby," he ordered, and I took a few deep breaths to calm my body.

"You're gonna need to back off, honey," I rasped. "You keep hitting that, I'm gonna explode."

He shifted and buried himself deeper, taking a second to smile at me before he slammed into me again, over and over, finally shifting again and hitting me exactly where I needed him, and I came. Spectacularly.

Merrick wasn't far behind, rolling us to our sides before realizing my leg was still stretched up his body.

"Fuck, sorry."

I grinned. "It's all good, Tweety."

He moved so I could reposition myself, and I draped myself across his chest.

"Love how flexible you are," he said, kissing me gently.

"You do?"

"I can go deep."

I chuckled. "Yeah, you can."

"How's your arm?"

"It's good," I said.

"And the other bruises?"

"I'm good, honey. I'm going to soak later, though."

"Want me to wash your hair?"

I grinned. "Yes, please."

He kissed me again. "I'll go get a baggie for your arm."

"Thanks, honey."

He slid out of bed and I headed to the bathroom to start the tub.

* * *

"I hate it," I complained, sliding to the floor in front of the mirrored wall.

It was the day after Merrick and I had ordered a new sofa, and it had been way too long between dance sessions for me, which meant, every step I took sucked. Bad.

"Why?" Grace asked. "I think it's great."

I shook my head. "It's not good enough, Grace. I know it, you know it, *Cassidy* will know it."

She sighed.

"You need a partner," Lily said, sitting beside me.

Lily Quinn just so happened to be Cassidy's daughter-in-law. She was married to Maverick, who was one of Merrick's Dog brothers, along with his father, Ace.

"Do you know anyone?" I asked, hopefully.

"No, not really. The two guys I used to dance with have gone to other companies in California."

"Rude," I said.

"Right?" Lily lamented.

"I bet Cassidy would know someone," Grace said.

I shook my head. "I want to work this out myself."

"What about Finch?" Lily said.

"What about me?" Merrick asked, walking through the door.

"Standing in as partner."

"Nope," he said, with an emphasis on the 'p.'

"It's fine," I said.

"It's for Remington, Merr," Grace provided, and he frowned.

"You need a partner?" he asked.

"If I want to do what I need to, yes. But I need someone trained. It's fine, honey."

"He's trained," Grace said.

"Grace," Merrick warned.

"He is," Lily added. "He took two years during football. And Cass uses him sometimes when she's desperate."

"Enough," Merrick snapped. "I'm not wearing tights for anyone. Sorry, baby, but it ain't happenin'."

"You wouldn't need to wear tights," Grace said.

"You really wouldn't," I said. "I just need an anchor. Someone strong enough to lift me."

He dropped his head back and hissed out, "Jesus," to the ceiling.

Grace clapped her hands. "That's a yes."

"That's not what I heard," I said, but studied him, once again hopeful.

He met my eyes. "I'll do it."

I couldn't love him more in this moment.

"You will?"

"Yeah, baby, I will. I have no clue if I'll do any good, but I can be your anchor."

I jumped to my feet and threw myself against him, kissing his neck as he wrapped his arms around me and hugged me close. "Thank you."

"It'll be worth it just for that," he whispered.

I leaned back and smiled up at him. "Can we work on something now?"

"What about your bruises and your arm?"

"They're healing, and I've been hurt worse in shows and had to dance through it. Well, maybe not the arm, but I don't need my arm for this routine," I pressed. "Please?"

He shrugged. "Sure."

I kissed him again and took his hand to pull him to the barre and faced the mirror. "I need you to stand like this."

I gave him a quick lesson on how to hold his core and how I needed him to catch me, then guided him to the middle of the room. "Promise me you'll catch me. Even if it's not pretty."

He smiled. "Not gonna let you fall, Rem."

I bit my lip, then nodded and walked to the opposite side of the room. I moved into a plié, then up on my feet to relevé before stepping into glissades, repeating those steps as I made my way to Merrick. He watched me closely, and when I sped up slightly, I saw him lock his body at the same time as he loosened his arms, ready to catch me.

Then I was flying.

Into his arms, then into the air as he lifted me above his head and dropped me toward the floor, holding me locked to him, my feet to the sky, before lifting me again and setting me gently back on my toes.

He was perfect. A hell of a lot better than someone who'd only done two years of training.

I heard a whoop and a holler, then multiple whoops and hollers, and I faced the sound as Merrick slid his arm around my waist. Flea and Maverick had arrived and were in the corner waiting with Grace and Lily, clapping like we were rock stars and I grinned big as I hugged Merrick tight. "You misled me on your level of 'training,'" I accused.

He laughed. "Well, now you know."

"You're the prettiest fuckin' ballerina I ever seen, Finch," Flea joked.

"Hey," Grace snapped, smacking his arm.

Flea laughed and wrapped his arms around her. "Sorry, second prettiest."

I gripped Merrick's cut and stood on pointe to kiss him gently. "That was perfect. Exactly what I needed."

"Yeah?"

"Yes. Will you do that with me for my audition?"

"Yeah, baby. Whatever you need."

"I love you," I whispered, kissing him again.

"Love you, too. Wanna get some food?"

"Yes! I'm starving."

I joined Lily and Grace and we pulled sweats on over our leotards and tights, then followed the men out to the vehicles. It was raining so no one had their bikes, which was a bummer, but we headed to a local restaurant and spent the rest of the evening laughing with our friends.

It had been the perfect day.

* * *

"Jesus," Merrick hissed as he pushed in deeper.

I smiled, loving the power I had over him right now. As promised, he'd bought lube. Lots of it and I was currently on my side pressing against his extremely hard cock, trying to take him all the way.

"Rem, you need to slow down."

"I want you in."

He pushed again, and I gripped his arm anchored around my waist.

"Okay, maybe a little slower," I rasped, swallowing.

"It's too much."

"No, it's not," I countered. "Don't stop, honey. Please."

He kept me tight to him, his front to my back, and pressed in again. "You okay?" he asked.

"I'm fine, honey," I promised, and he buried himself a little further, while I tried not to come. Even though it was a little uncomfortable, I was ridiculously turned on. "Fuck me, Tweety."

"Don't want to hurt you, Rem."

"You're not hurting me."

"Fuck, you feel so good."

"So do you," I whispered.

He moved slowly, and I tried to rock, but he slapped

my ass in response.

"If you're trying to get me to slow down, slapping me like that isn't helping," I ground out. "It just riles me more."

"Baby, settle," he ordered. "My dick is buried somewhat deep and tight and you making me laugh is just gonna rile *me* more."

He reached over my legs and slid a finger into my pussy, keeping his thumb connected to my clit and then finally began to move. I moved with him, my orgasm building hard and fast…like usual, but this one was far more intense, and I shuddered as a climax washed over me, quickly followed by another.

"Fuck," he rasped, gently pulling out of me. "God damn, baby. Even part way in, it was amazing."

"That was so, so good."

"That's beyond an understatement," he said. "If dancing with you means that? I'm in every day."

I chuckled. "Well, let's see how I feel tomorrow, and go from there."

"Are you sore?" he asked, suddenly concerned.

"Not really, but you're the only one I've let in, so…"

He grinned, kissing me gently. "That means everything to me, baby."

"To me too. I love you more than you will ever know."

"I'm getting an idea, but it still doesn't come close to what I feel for you."

I rolled my eyes. "It's not a competition."

"Well, if it was, I'd win."

"Oh my god, you so wouldn't."

He slid off the bed and headed for the bathroom. "So would."

I followed and turned on the shower. "You gonna lather me up, cowboy?"

"Lather, rile, whatever my queen needs."

I grinned. "Correct answer, peasant."

SEVENTEEN

Remington

T HE FOLLOWING SATURDAY, the Dogs were hosting a family get-together, which meant I would meet the rest of Merrick's "brothers." I was nervous. I didn't really know why, but I felt like this was a huge deal and I was going to be under a microscope.

I was in our bedroom when I heard raised male voices from the family room and headed toward the sound.

"Goddammit, Merrick, you could have been in real trouble."

"Dad, the asshole beat the shit out of Remington, then pulled a knife on me. It was self-defense."

"You shot him in the heart at close range. He was on the floor."

Oh my god!

"Actually shot him twice in the chest before he was on

the floor, Dad. He kept coming. He was falling as I shot."

"Do you know how hard it is to get a shot dead center, particularly when one is falling?"

Merrick didn't respond, so I made my way into the room. He caught my eye and sighed, holding his arm out to me. "Come meet my dad, Rem."

Merrick's father turned, and I forced a smile. Good gravy, they looked alike. Merrick had hazel eyes, where his father had blue, and his dad was mostly silver-haired and obviously older, but I got a glimpse into what Merrick would look like as he aged, and I liked what I saw.

"Mr. Lundy," I said, holding my hand out. "It's nice to meet you."

He shook my hand and smiled, so much like Merrick. "It's nice to meet you too, sweetheart. Call me Ryan. Heard you had a rough go of it in Savannah."

I nodded as Merrick wrapped an arm around me and pulled me close. "It wasn't fun."

"I understand Nadia Popov is being tried for attempted murder."

"Really?" I asked.

Merrick gave me a gentle squeeze. "We don't need to talk about that right now."

"Oh, I don't know about that, Tweety. I think now's a great time to talk about it."

"I'll fill you in later," Merrick said with another squeeze.

"*Or*, your dad can fill me in now, since he appears to have the most updated information."

Merrick's body locked, and I knew in that moment he was keeping stuff from me.

"Well, I need to get going," Ryan said. "Dinner next week?"

"Sure," Merrick replied. "Sounds great."

He separated himself from me and walked his dad to the door, then faced me.

"What aren't you telling me?" I asked.

"Babe, it doesn't touch you. Get your shoes on and we'll go. You're on my bike."

I pointed to my arm. "It already touched me, Merrick. Literally. What's going on?"

He dragged his hands through his hair. "They're investigating my involvement. Whether or not it was a clean shoot."

I gasped. "Oh my god. Are you going to jail?"

"No."

"Are you sure?"

"Yeah. It was a clean shoot. Self-defense."

I closed the distance between us and gripped his cut. "Are. You. Sure?"

He stroked my cheek. "Yeah, baby. Dad's helping, as is Jaxon…he's F.B.I. I'm covered."

I dropped my head to his chest. "If I lost you…" I couldn't even finish the thought. It was too much.

He lifted my chin and kissed me gently. "You're not gonna lose me, Eeyore. Go get your shoes and we'll head out."

I studied him for a few seconds before grabbing my boots and meeting him by the front door. After donning a leather jacket, he led me to his bike, stowed my purse in a saddlebag, then helped me with my helmet. It was a rare dry day for Portland, so I was looking forward to this ride. Particularly since it was my first time on a motorcycle.

"Hold on tight, Rem. Lean when I lean, and if you need me, pat my chest."

I nodded. "Okay."

He climbed on, then helped me on the back and we were off.

It was magical, and a little scary…but mostly magical. Feeling the hum of the engine in my nether regions while I was wrapped around my man was heady. By the time we pulled into the compound parking lot, I wanted to drag

Merrick into a closet somewhere and ease the ache.

"You good?" he asked, pushing down the kickstand.

"Other than horny as hell, yes," I admitted, pulling off my helmet.

He held me as I climbed off the bike, then got off himself. "You wanna take a minute?"

"Can we?"

He raised an eyebrow, setting our helmets on the bike seats. "Of course we can. We'll go in the back."

I bit my lip and nodded. "Let's hurry."

He grabbed my bag out of the saddlebag, then took my hand and guided me in through the back of the building and upstairs.

The Dogs of Fire compound was at the back of Big Ernie's, an autobody shop, and much more prison-like than I expected. I missed the coolness of the Savannah barn, but kept my opinion to myself as Merrick unlocked a grey door and pushed it open. Turning on the light, he covered my mouth with his and kicked the door shut.

"You good with a quickie?" he asked, pushing the leather jacket from my shoulders, letting it fall to the floor.

"I'm not the one who constantly gabs while fucking, Tweety, so maybe you should ask yourself that," I joked.

He chuckled as he tugged my T-shirt over my head and cupped my breasts. "Sorry, girls, no play time for you, we don't have time."

I swatted his hands away, and knelt before him, my hands going to the waistband of his jeans. "God, you are so *wordy*."

He chuckled. "You gonna let me put my dick in your pussy?"

"In a minute," I retorted, tugging his pants down, freeing his cock. "Mmm, my precious."

"Does that make me lord of the cock rings?"

"Look, if you want our roleplaying to move into LARPing territory, I'm going to need to expand my wardrobe to include some sexy cloaks.”

“Don’t make me laugh when you’re about to blow me.”

I grinned and ran my tongue up the length, before wrapping my lips around the tip, then taking him all the way to the back of my throat.

Unfortunately for me, he was having none of it, and I was dragged up in the form of his hands in my armpits and thrown gently onto the bed. My boots, jeans, and panties were ripped from my body and his face was buried in my pussy forthwith, and I was hit with an orgasm without warning. “Merrick,” I panted out as my climax washed over me.

Before I’d crested, he was inside me and he was pushing me toward another. I slid my legs over his hips, digging my heels into his ass and taking him deeper. Merrick kissed me, sliding his hand between us and fingering my clit as he slammed into me over and over.

“Get there, Tweety,” I begged, and he thrust a little faster before letting out a grunt and falling over me and kissing my neck.

“You need more?” he asked, and I chuckled.

“Always, but I’m good for a few hours.”

He slid out of me and duck walked to the bathroom, his jeans still around his ankles. I sat up just as someone pounded on the door. “Merrick!” Grace called. “Are you in there?”

Merrick put his finger to his lips, and I nodded.

“Babe, he’s not here,” Flea said.

“His bike’s here, honey. He must be here.”

“Maybe he wants to be alone.”

“And miss family night?”

Merrick dropped his head back and whispered out a series of curses, then he slid his phone out of his pocket and glanced at the screen. Shaking his head, his thumbs flew over the screen and I figured he was texting someone.

"Well, hurry up," Grace called through the door and I shoved my face in a pillow to laugh.

"Jesus," Merrick hissed. "I suppose we should clean up and get downstairs."

I smiled up at him. "One more?"

He went for the button on his jeans. "Fuck, yes."

* * *

We made our way downstairs almost thirty minutes later, and Grace made a beeline for us, followed by Flea who was giving Merrick a look of apology, and a bottle of beer.

"Gross," Grace said, and hugged me, then Merrick. "And that's all I'm gonna say on the subject."

"You didn't have to say anything, sissy," Merrick said, taking the beer from Flea with a chin lift. Biker speak for 'Thanks.'

"Have you met me?" she retorted.

"There is that." Merrick took a swig of beer and wrapped his arm around my shoulders.

"So, your man brings mine a beer, but you don't hook your girl up with wine?" I accused.

"I am the worst friend ever." Grace laid her hand over her heart. "Let me fix that immediately."

She took my hand and tugged me away from Merrick and we headed to the kitchen.

"Hey, Gracie." A gorgeous blonde pulled her in for a hug.

"Did you just get here?"

The blonde nodded and grinned at me. "I'm Poppy."

"She's my bestie when I claim her," Grace said.

"Hi. I'm Remington."

"Oh, you're with Finch."

I chuckled. "Guilty."

"Sid adores you," she said.

"Sid?"

"Hatch," Grace provided.

"Sorry," Poppy said with a chuckle. "He's technically my step-dad, but I've called him my stand-in-dad forever, so he's Sid."

"That's really sweet," I said.

Poppy grinned. "Well, he's sweet."

"Who's sweet?" Hatch asked, walking into the room.

"You."

"Fuck, baby girl, don't ruin my street cred." He pulled her in for a hug and kissed her head. "Where's Sparky?"

She shrugged. "Somewhere."

I would find out Sparky was her super gorgeous, super protective fiancé and he just so happened to be Hatch's nephew.

Hatch hugged Grace, then faced me. "You doin' okay?"

I nodded. "On the mend."

"Good." He smiled, then turned to Poppy. "Your mom wants wine, so I best get her wine."

"We're here for that too," Grace said, and walked into the pantry, returning with two bottles of red.

Once Hatch left with a solo cup of wine, Poppy leaned against the island and sipped hers. "How's Alamo doing?"

"Merrick said he's good."

"Jasmine was probably totally freaked."

"Right?" Grace said. "If Flea got cut, I'd rage, then cry."

"I'd pay to see you rage," Flea said, walking in behind her.

"Cage match," Merrick said, and I tugged on his cut. "Be nice."

He grinned and wrapped an arm around me. "No promises."

Hatch walked back into the kitchen and gave Merrick a chin lift. "Got a minute?"

"Yeah," he said. He gave me a gentle squeeze, then followed Hatch out of the room.

Finch

Hatch led me into his office at the back of the compound and shut the door, waving to a chair across from his desk. "Have a seat."

I lowered myself into the chair as he sat behind his desk and settled his arms on it, leaning forward. "We need to get some shit sorted."

I frowned. "Like?"

"Like the fact you hauled off and broke Vitaly's knee-cap, then shot him in the heart."

I held up three fingers. "*Three* times in the heart."

"Don't be flippant, Finch."

"What are you trying to say here?"

"This is not our club, son. We might rough some asshole up, but we don't murder them."

"It wasn't fucking murder!" I snapped.

He studied me. "Break it down."

I dragged my hands down my face. "Already talked to the cops and my dad. What else do you need to know?"

"I wanna know the truth."

I leaned forward. "What makes you think I haven't told the truth?"

"Because I'm aware that *you're* aware, our club doesn't do this," he said. "And you and I don't fuckin' lie to each other."

I sighed, sitting back in the chair. He was right. We don't lie to each other. So I told him. Everything. The fact I wrapped the asshole's hand around his knife and staged the scene. What I said to him before I shot him in the heart. All of it.

Hatch leaned back and listened. No comments, no outward expression or reaction, just total silence. When I was finished, I felt like the weight of the world had been lifted from my shoulders, and my surrogate father leaned forward again. "So. Clean shot."

"Clean shot, Hatch. Swear to Christ. The animal had Remington tied down and was torturing her, but I did not lose control. I knew exactly what I was doing."

He nodded. "Doc said local PD and F.B.I. agreed the action was in self-defense."

"Yeah?"

"You were fuckin' lucky Dalton Moore was there to take credit for the capture of Sokolov. He covered your asses, even though it was somewhat murky."

"There was nothing murky about it, Hatch. I just wish I'd fucking got Vitaly's uncle too."

"Yeah, well, he's goin' somewhere he can't reach his cohorts, so it's a win-win in Dalton's opinion."

"I thought he wasn't in the F.B.I. anymore," I countered.

"He's still a consultant, and specifically involved in cases he wasn't able to close as an official agent. He's splitting time between Savannah and Scotland for a while."

"So, what does that mean for me?" I asked.

"You're clear, Finch. As is the club."

I relaxed.

"But we need to address the bigger issue here."

"There is no issue," I countered.

He raised an eyebrow. "Bud, there's an issue."

"Remington's safe, he's dead, there's not a fucking issue, Hatch."

I rose to my feet, but before I reached the door, Hatch's hand landed on my shoulder.

"We're not done."

I faced him and crossed my arms. "Just fucking spit it out, Hatch."

"When you saw Remington lying there, broken and bruised, what were you feelin'?"

"Rage."

"That all?"

"Yeah," I lied, the memories of Grace's tiny body covered with my mother's blood, bone, and brain matter flashing through my mind.

Hatch's hand went to my shoulder again. "Nothin' else?"

I shook my head but couldn't look him in the eye.

"You haven't fully dealt with all the trauma with your mom, Merrick. Think you need to do that."

"I'm not talking to a shrink. Did that right after. It didn't help."

"I hear ya. But you gotta talk to someone. Like your dad."

"Not talking to my dad about this, Hatch."

"Then me," he said quietly. "Or Maisie. Or Remington. Or the fuckin' moon, for all I care. You keep this shit locked up tight, it'll blow…worse than the Vitaly thing."

"I get it. No bringing dishonor to the club."

"You really think that's what I'm sayin'?" he asked, squeezing my shoulder. "'Cause if it is, you fuckin' walk out that door right now."

I shook my head.

"Right. So. You gotta work it out. I love you like a son, Merr. Whatever you need, I'm here, but if you get yourself killed or locked up, I'm gonna fuckin' lose my shit."

I shifted, trying to loosen Hatch's grip on me. He didn't budge. He just stared at me with his dad eyes. No judgement, just concern.

"She was so fucking little," I rasped.

"Remington?"

I shook my head. "Gracie."

"Yeah."

"She looked like something outta Carrie."

"She did," he said.

"Mom was gonna kill her."

He squeezed my shoulder again.

"I should have been there."

"You were a kid. Nothin' you coulda done," Hatch said.

"Yeah. But I'm never letting anything like that happen again. To Grace *or* Rem."

"Got your back on that one," he said, and pulled me in for a hug. It was quick, but it was fatherly, then he slapped me on my back and pulled away. "Gonna give you a few."

"Thanks."

Hatch walked out the door and I sat in the chair I'd just vacated, dropping my head as I thought about everything Hatch had said.

Small hands wrapped around my arms and I opened my eyes to find my sister kneeling in front of me. "Hey."

I forced a smile. "Hey, sissy."

"You okay?"

"Getting there."

"Do you want to talk about it?"

"No."

"Is this about Mom?"

"Indirectly," I said.

"It's about me?"

I took her hand and squeezed. "Yeah, baby sister. It's kind of about you."

"What happened?"

"It doesn't matter."

"Did you get in trouble?"

I chuckled. "No, sissy, I didn't get in trouble."

She let out a sigh of relief. "I thought Hatch was going to give you a lecture like Dad does."

"No."

"Are we okay?"

I frowned. "Why wouldn't we be?"

She shrugged, her face so much like our mother's, looking vulnerable and sad. "Because you've been so distant. I mean, before Remi."

"I'm sorry, Gracie." I kissed her forehead, standing and

pulling her up for a hug. "I'll fix that."

"I'd really like that." She wrapped her arms around me and squeezed. "Remi's a little worried about you, but Hatch told me to come get you." She smiled up at me. "I'm glad he did."

"Me too," I said and gave her one more squeeze before following her back to the party.

Remington made her way to me and took my hand. "Can I borrow you for a bit?"

"Yeah, baby."

She led me back the way I came and pulled me into Hatch's office.

* * *

Remington

"What happened?" she asked, closing the door.

I filled her in on my conversation with Hatch, leaving out the details about what actually happened in Savannah.

She grinned and gripped my cut, standing on her tiptoes to kiss me. "I like your surrogate dad."

I chuckled. "Me too."

"But I love you."

"I love you too."

"I will always listen, honey. You won't look weak in my eyes if you're having a tough time with what happened. It's trauma."

"I know."

I patted his chest. "Do you know in here, though?"

He settled his hand over mine. "Yeah, baby, I know in here."

"Good. Now, kiss me, then I want you to get me tipsy and fuck me."

His eyes darkened, and he smiled as he covered my mouth with his. Then he took me back to the party and got me tipsy before taking me to his room and fucking me.

EIGHTEEN

Remington

ABOUT SIX WEEKS later, I was soaking in the tub after one hell of an audition with Cassidy and replaying the routine in my head. Merrick had totally stepped up for me, and if I wasn't chosen to be part of the company, then it wasn't because of anything we did. I'd had my cast removed four days ago, so I'd only gotten one practice in without it before my audition.

"You got a delivery," Merrick said, leaning over me.

"A good one?"

"I'll get it. Stay put."

I stayed put, but I did shift so I was facing the door. Merrick walked in carrying a huge bouquet of flowers. Well, I should say, the flowers grew legs and walked in, since I couldn't see his face.

"Who are those from?" I asked as he set them on the

counter.

"Want me to read the card?"

"Yes, please."

He pulled the card out of the envelope and read, *"These flowers don't match the grace and beauty with which you danced today. I am so proud and happy to offer you a place in our ballet company. I have emailed you with details. Much love, Cassidy."*

I let out a squeal and jumped up, sloshing water over the side of the tub.

"Babe, careful, you'll slip," Merrick growled as he reached out to me.

I took his hand and he helped me out, then I toweled off quickly, making a run for my laptop, despite being buck-naked. I pulled up my email and saw one from Cassidy, so I opened it and scanned through it really quick.

"Oh my god, honey, it's like twice what I was offered at PBC."

"Is that good?" he asked from our closet.

"Yes," I said and made my way to him. "What are you doing in the closet?"

I pushed open the door and found him on one knee a gorgeous antique ring nestled in a velvet box in his hand. I covered my mouth with my hands.

"I love you, Rem. Will you marry me?"

I blinked back tears as I nodded. "Yes. A thousand times yes."

He grinned, standing and picking me up to carry me to the bed. He dropped me on the mattress gently, then set my laptop aside and stretched out beside me, slipping the ring on my finger.

I held my hand up and hummed in appreciation. A large diamond, probably two carats, was surrounded by smaller diamonds, and a filigree pattern on the white gold band. "It's amazing."

"It was my grandmother's."

I turned my head to look at him. "Her engagement ring?"

"Yeah."

"Oh, wow. And she's okay with it?"

I'd met his grandmother a few weeks ago at a family dinner, but the get-together had been a little tense. Merrick's dad and his lady friend weren't getting along, and quite frankly, she was kind of a bitch to him. Merrick's grandmother had laid into her, then asked Flea and Grace to take her home. That had been the end of the get-together.

"Grams adores you honey."

"She does?"

He slid his hand to my neck. "Were you *not* at the same dinner as me?"

"I just remember her going off on your dad's girlfriend. Your grandmother and I didn't get a chance to talk, so how would she know she likes me?"

"She clocked you within five minutes."

I rolled my eyes. "Really?"

"Yep. She loves you. Trust me. She gave me the big ring to give you."

I chuckled. "That's the test?"

"Hell, yeah. If she didn't like you, she would have given me the garnet ring she's also hanging onto for me or Grace."

"I like garnet."

"It's fake."

I wrinkled my nose. "Oh, no fakes for me."

"Exactly," he said, and kissed me. "Let's get naughty."

"Get the lube," I said, and he laughed.

"And this is why I'm the luckiest man alive."

"Because I let you do butt stuff to me?"

"Yes," he hissed out, now laughing uncontrollably. "So fucking romantic."

I straddled him, leaning down to kiss him. "Gonna

show you just how romantic when you stop laughing."

He stopped immediately and flipped me onto my back, running his nose against mine. "Gonna feast on your pussy first, then I'll fuck you hard."

I nodded, my body shivering with anticipation. "Okay, fiancé."

"Fucking love that, Rem."

I smiled. "Me too."

He kissed his way down my body, sliding off the bed to remove his clothes before kneeling between my legs and covering my mound with his mouth, sucking gently, then moving to my clit.

Just as things started to get good, someone pounded on his door. I whimpered when I lost his mouth and he sat up. The pounding started again, and he snapped out a curse before pulling on his jeans and stalking out of the room. I dressed quickly and followed, pissed that my perfect engagement had been ruined by some asshole we weren't expecting. I walked out to the living room to find Merrick facing off with a very familiar man.

"Daddy? What are you doing here?"

"Did your mother steal your money?"

"What?" I asked, glancing at Merrick, hoping he didn't have his gun handy.

"Did your mother steal your money?" he repeated. "It's a simple question, Remington."

"Yes."

"Goddammit."

I gasped. My father never swore. Ever.

"You didn't know?" I whispered.

"You asking me that question wounds me, Remi."

I blinked back tears.

He shook his head. "Had I known, I would have made it right."

"She said it was all for you," I said.

"She lied."

Of course she did.

Merrick wrapped an arm around me. "You want him to leave?"

"No. Daddy, this is Merrick. My fiancé. Honey, my dad, Walter."

My dad held his hand out and Merrick hesitated, but took his hand after a few tense seconds.

"I'm going to sort this out, honey," Dad said.

"Merrick already took care of it," I said.

"I know. But I'm going to pay you back what she stole."

"Dad, it's fine. I don't need it," I said.

He scowled. "That's not the point, Remi. It's your money. She had no right to take it."

"Okay," I whispered.

He stroked my face. "I'm going to make this right, baby. Your mother will never hurt you again."

I wrapped my arms around him and dropped my cheek to his chest. "Thanks, Daddy."

"I'm sorry I wasn't there for you more," he said, and stroked my back. "And I'm sorry I didn't protect you against Thomas."

I looked up at him. "Are you dying?"

He shook his head and smiled. "No. But I've been asleep nigh on thirty years and that ends today." He kept his arm around me and looked at Merrick. "Thanks for doing what I should have done. I appreciate it."

Merrick nodded, looking as bewildered as I felt.

Dad looked back to me. "I hope you'll still allow me to give you away, baby. Regardless, you figure out what you want, and I'll pay for everything. Just send me the bills."

I burst into tears and held him tight, nodding into his chest. "Okay, Daddy."

"I'm here for a few more days. Will you allow me to take you both to dinner tomorrow night?"

"That would be great," Merrick said. "Thanks."

"I'm going to go ahead and go, honey. We'll talk to-morrow."

"Okay," I said, and released him. He shook Merrick's hand again, then left us and I fell onto our new micro-suede sofa, dropping my face in my hands.

Merrick kneeled in front of me, tugging my hands away. "You okay?"

"I thought he was part of it."

"Yeah, baby."

"Do you believe him?" I asked.

"The important question is, do you?"

I met his eyes. "Yes. But does that make me an idiot?"

"No, Eeyore, it doesn't. If you want, though, I can have Booker dig deeper and find out."

I nodded. "Yes, please."

"Okay, honey. I'll take care of that tomorrow."

I wiped my cheeks and smiled. "Thank you. Now, we have some lube to destroy."

"Shit, baby, you sure you're up to that?"

"Hells, yes. I demand satisfaction, sir," I said and went super southern on him, rising to my feet and heading to-ward the bedroom.

"Babe."

I turned on him and slid my hand to his waistband. "I want butt sex."

He dropped his head back and laughed. "Holy shit, ba-by, you're crazy."

"You love crazy."

"I *do* love crazy," he said, bending and lifting me over his shoulder like a sack of potatoes.

"Tweety!" I squealed, wrapping my arms around his waist as I hung upside down.

His hand landed on my butt and he squeezed my right cheek as he walked me into the bedroom. I shivered at his touch and when he dropped me on the bed, I yanked my clothes off as quickly as I could, rewarded with him burying himself deep inside of me as he kissed me gently.

"I love you, Remington Aultman Charles, soon to be Lundy."

"I love you, too, Merrick Tweety Lundy, soon to be Charles."

He chuckled, and his dick pulsed inside of me as he did. "Mmm, I like that."

"I'm gonna do stuff you like better in a second."

"Yay," I whispered.

"Can't wait to marry you, baby."

I smiled, stroking his face. "Me too."

Merrick kissed me again and then made love to me with more gentleness than I expected, but it was exactly what I needed.

I was cherished, which made me free.

EPILOGUE

Remington

Three years later…

"**Y**OU ARE BEAUTIFUL," Merrick whispered from the side of the stage.

I grinned, kissing him, careful not to smear my makeup. "Thanks, honey."

"Break a leg."

I nodded, and my cue sounded. I was the Sugar Plum Fairy in the Nutcracker. Admittedly, this ballet was not my favorite, but it brought in a lot of money for the company I was totally committed to. I loved my job and every spring, I was given the opportunity to assist in the choreography of originally scored music. A big draw for musicians and dancers alike, and one of the things that made Cassidy's company *the* conservatory to attend.

I'd asked if I could choreograph something by myself this spring, knowing that eventually, I wanted to have babies, and pregnant ballerinas weren't in high-demand, but if I did well choreographing unique pieces, I could work forever…in theory, anyway.

Life had taken an amazing turn. Our wedding had been a total fairy tale, held at an historic mansion in Portland, and as promised, my father had paid for everything regarding the wedding. He'd also paid me back the almost two-million my mother had stolen, right after he divorced her and left her destitute. In truth, she wasn't really destitute, but she certainly tried to make everyone believe she was.

Daddy gave her the four-thousand square foot home on the lake, along with a car and a ten-thousand a month alimony payment. She was doing just fine in my opinion.

My brother, Dawson, and I had cut all ties with her, and we built a whole new and amazing relationship with my Dad. He'd cut back his hours at his office as well, so he had more time to 'hang' with Dawson and fly here whenever I needed or wanted him to be here.

Like tonight. He and my brother were in the front-row and clapping the loudest. I smiled as I moved to the center of the stage, finding my dad in the audience and lowering my head slightly. He gave me his two-gun pointing fingers which signaled to me he saw me nod. It was our little ritual every time he watched me perform and I cherished it.

My family was, in fact, staying with us. We'd bought a home in Vancouver, and it was larger than we really needed, but Merrick promised we'd fill it soon. Plus, it came in handy at Christmas when my dad, brother, and whichever girl he was with came for the holidays. This year, however, Dawson was single, and Christmas would be spent at Hatch and Maisie's home.

The club always did a Christmas Eve party for the neighborhood foster kids. Flick dressed up as Santa every year, but Dad had offered up his services should Flick ever need a break. Dad was still waiting for his 'shot.'

New Year's this year would be in Savannah. Alamo had recovered completely, and he and Jasmine had insisted we come this year and party with the Savannah chapter. In fact, most of the Portland chapter would be joining us, so I couldn't wait to go home for a week.

Every year, I spent the anniversary of Michelle's death giving blood in her memory, along with every single one of the Dogs. I'd done the swab thingy, as had Merrick and several of his brothers, but I had yet to give bone marrow. I was on the list and ready to go should I ever be a match for someone, so giving blood helped me feel like I wasn't just sitting on my thumbs.

I couldn't believe how my life had changed in such a short amount of time. I had never felt so safe and cherished. Ever. Merrick had done that for me. He'd pursued me and loved me with a passion I never expected.

He was everything and as I danced off the stage, I wrapped myself around him and kissed him.

"You were perfect, baby," he whispered.

"All because of you."

That wasn't hyperbole. He helped me practice, acting as my anchor and my partner in both dance and life.

"You did all the work, baby. I just made sure you didn't fall."

I cupped his face. "That's everything, Tweety."

He smiled. "Love you, honey."

"I love you, too."

We stood in the wings as the ballet finished and then it was time to take a bow and Merrick waited for me once again. As I curtsied, I turned to find him smiling at me and I said a quick prayer of thanks for the man who set me free.

Life was better than I could have ever hoped for.

Hello, lovelies. I hope you've enjoyed Road to Freedom.

This story is incredibly close to my heart, as Jack and I have a good friend named Michelle who is fighting one hell of a battle with cancer. Things are dire unless she gets life-saving stem cells.

If you'd like to find out about donating bone marrow or stem cells, please visit www.dkms.org for more information! The more people who donate, the more people can be a match for the cure.

Help me give a big "FUCK YOU" to cancer!

New York Times & USA Today Bestselling Author Piper Davenport writes from a place of passion and intrigue, combining elements of romance and suspense with strong modern-day heroes and heroines.

She currently resides in the Pacific Northwest with her author husband, Jack Davenport, and an obnoxious YorkiePoo named Pepper who may or may not be an international spy.

Like Piper's FB page and get to know her!
(www.facebook.com/piperdavenport)